"Have you ever fired a gun?"

"No." Nor did she want to. Although she had a feeling she might have to.

"You should know that I always have one on me." He opened his jacket to reveal a holstered weapon. "As a ranger, it was my job to go into an area and clear it of enemy risks. It taught me never to be afraid. Fear is your worst enemy in battle."

She suspected he didn't fear anything or anyone. He'd swooped in to save her, facing death to protect someone he didn't even know.

She felt a rush of gratitude. So much for keeping a level head around him. She stared up into his face. "Thanks for helping me, Colton. I don't know what would have happened to me..." She fought back tears.

His eyes met hers. "I'll keep you safe, Laura. I promise."

How long had it been since she'd been able to trust a man?

And why did she want so badly to believe in this one?

Virginia Vaughan is a born-and-raised Mississippi girl. She is blessed to come from a large Southern family, and her fondest memories include listening to stories recounted around the dinner table. She was a lover of books from a young age, devouring tales of romance, danger and love. She soon started writing them herself. You can connect with Virginia through her website, virginiavaughanonline.com, or through the publisher.

Books by Virginia Vaughan

Love Inspired Suspense

Rangers Under Fire

Yuletide Abduction
Reunion Mission
Ranch Refuge

No Safe Haven

RANCH REFUGE

VIRGINIA VAUGHAN

HARLEQUIN® LOVE INSPIRED® SUSPENSE

Recycling programs
for this product may
not exist in your area.

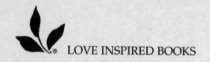 LOVE INSPIRED BOOKS

ISBN-13: 978-0-373-44763-3

Ranch Refuge

Copyright © 2016 by Virginia Vaughan

www.Harlequin.com

Printed in U.S.A.

Surely the arm of the Lord is not too short to save,
nor His ear too dull to hear.
—Isaiah 59:1

This book is dedicated to my Lord and Savior Jesus Christ. You have seen me through the ups and downs of life, always preparing me for what is to come and helping me to stand strong against the storms.

Also, to my sister, Lisa, for your nursing expertise that greatly added to the authenticity of this story.

ONE

Laura Jackson quickened her pace as she headed for her car. The parking lot had been full of activity when she'd arrived for work at the River City Medical Center at seven this morning, but now, after a nearly sixteen-hour shift, the employee parking lot was all but deserted. Her car sat in the back of the lot, along with a handful of other vehicles of shift workers, abandoned for the night.

The streetlamps illuminated a scattered area of the dark lot, but her car was on the back row, past the safety of the bright lights. Although she'd initially toyed with the idea of calling the security office for an escort, she'd opted against it because she hadn't felt like waiting for them to arrive. She was ready to get home, into her own bed, and try to get some rest. Wiping away a trickle of sweat from her brow, Laura hiked her backpack up on her shoulder as she crossed the parking lot. The Louisiana summer night was muggy and added to the lethargy she was already feeling. As an ER nurse, she was accustomed to the long shifts at the hospital, used to operating on only a few hours of sleep, but lately something else had been keeping her up, even on her nights off work.

She stopped short when a man stepped from between two rows of cars. He nodded at her, then leaned against the back of a truck, seemingly paying her no more attention. He was tall and good-looking, dressed in boots and jeans, and, even without a hat on his head, she could tell he was a cowboy. Laura continued past him, her senses on high alert for anything suspicious. As she walked past, she felt his eyes follow her, watching as she neared her car.

She readied her keys, prepared to do battle against him if necessary. She hated how her mind automatically moved toward evil intentions. A few weeks ago she might have smiled flirtatiously at the ruggedly handsome cowboy or confronted the man and demanded to know why he was lurking around the parking lot. But that was before the notes began…before the late-night visits from Chuck Randall and his goon squad… before she'd learned her father had done the unthinkable and promised loan sharks and bookies that Laura would cover his gambling debts. Was this cowboy one of those men who'd come to try to collect from her? She'd made herself clear. She wasn't paying. And she certainly wasn't interested in anything else Randall wanted from her, either.

Laura hit the button on her key fob and the lights on her car flashed. The cowboy moved, approaching her as headlights from another car in the lot flickered on and an engine revved loudly. She glanced at the car and saw it roar from its parking space and head her way.

Laura ran for her car, fumbling with her keys as the car sped toward her. The keys slipped through her fingers and hit the ground. She reached down to grab them and suddenly the cowboy was upon her, grabbing her arm and yanking her out of the way as the vehicle barreled past her.

Heart hammering in her chest, she hit the hood of a parked car with a thud and heard tires screeching behind her. She scrambled to her feet to see the cowboy pull a gun from his belt and aim it at the vehicle that was turning back toward them.

"The black pickup. Go now!" he shouted at her.

But Laura stood frozen, her eyes fixed on the vehicle barreling toward them.

"Laura, move now!" The cowboy punctuated his words by firing several shots at the approaching car.

Oh, God, help me!

She couldn't move. Paralyzed with fear, she could barely drag in her next breath. *This can't be happening... It just can't be.*

The cowboy sprinted in front of the oncoming car and grabbed her, once again pulling her out of the way just in time. He fired off a couple more shots as the vehicle screeched to a halt and then he gripped her arm and pulled her alongside him, his stride brisk and determined.

Laura tried to wrench herself free from his iron grasp as he headed toward the black pickup. Safety lessons rushed through her mind about getting into cars with strangers. She wouldn't go with these men…refused to let Randall win. "Let me go! What do you want with me? I don't have anything of value. Please! Just let me go."

He stopped and loosened his grip on her arm. His sharp features softened as he turned his warm, brown gaze to her, his eyes reflecting urgency. "I'm here to help you."

He was trying to rescue her. Maybe he wasn't one of Randall's men.

She looked at the car headed their way. Those were Randall's men. She was certain of it. But something about this stranger was different. She couldn't quite put her finger on what, but she saw more than strength in his square jaw and rock-hard physique. He had kindness in his face. Should she take a chance that he was one of the good guys? What choice did she really have?

He turned and fired toward the thugs again, hitting the windshield. The car swerved and smashed into a row of parked vehicles. "Get in the truck now," he commanded.

This time Laura did as she was told. She pulled open the passenger door and hurried inside. The cowboy slid into the driver's seat, gunned the engine and took off. Laura scrambled to find the seat belt and buckle it as they raced away from the would-be abduction.

She glanced back to see that the car was following them, but the cowboy—her rescuer now—pressed down hard on the accelerator and took off. His shoulders were tight, his jaw tense, yet his composure remained calm, cool, self-assured. She had the feeling he knew what he was doing and hadn't happened upon her by accident.

"Hold on," he instructed as he slammed on the brakes and turned the wheel, causing her to slide toward him.

The seat belt locked and she was yanked back in the opposite direction. Laura grabbed hold of the dash and tried to hang on. She wasn't complaining. Anything to keep free of Randall and his crazy obsession with her!

He gunned the engine again as the car came alongside them and the man in the backseat pulled out a gun.

"Get down!" her cowboy shouted, pushing her head down as shots rang out, dinging the truck and smashing the side window behind him. "Get on the floor!"

She unbuckled her seat belt and crouched on the floorboard as another shot whizzed past her and hit the passenger door.

He jerked the steering wheel and Laura heard metal crunch metal as he smashed into the side of the car, pushing it onto the shoulder and off the road before maneuvering the truck back onto the road, never once taking his foot off the accelerator.

Laura peered out the back window and saw the car on its side in a ditch and several men scrambling from the vehicle. "You did it. They're not chasing us."

He nodded curtly. "They'll regroup and be back."

Relief flooded her, then the startling realization that Randall had indeed sent men after her. She'd tried ignoring his threats and his advances, but it had done no good. If it wasn't for this handsome stranger, who knew where she might be now or what Randall would demand of her.

She stared at him as he concentrated on the road. His rugged jawline and profile seemed the embodiment of strength and courage. She wasn't afraid of this man, but she had no logical reason not to be. She didn't know him, yet she'd jumped into a truck with him. He'd swooped in like a hero in an action flick and rescued her.

"How did you know they were going to try to kidnap me?" she asked.

He turned his chocolate-brown eyes her way and her toes tingled at his gaze. However, his next words stopped her cold.

"Because I've been following you, Laura."

Colton didn't let up on the accelerator as he sped down the highway. He was less concerned about getting a speeding ticket than he was about getting Laura to safety.

She pressed herself against the passenger door, her hands shaking and her expression morphing from one of acceptance and gratitude to confusion and fear at his words.

"You…you were following me? Who are you? What do you want with me? And how do you know my name?" Her green eyes were wide with fear and her lips pressed hard into a line.

He gripped the steering wheel. "I don't want anything from you. I just saved your life. Those men were going to abduct you."

"And what were you doing? Why were you following me?"

"I was trying to help you." He saw the terror written across her pretty face and his gut clenched. He'd seen that expression too many times before during his deployment as an army ranger when his team had arrived out of the blue with guns and orders. But this wasn't

Afghanistan and he hadn't brandished his weapon at her. And he was no longer taking orders from anyone.

He'd met her father in Gamblers Anonymous and seen a man who was where he used to be. When Bill had confided that his daughter was in danger, Colton had offered his expertise. "I was only following you so I could be on the lookout. I figured Randall would send men after you. I just didn't know who or when. I wanted to be close by when they appeared. I'm not going to hurt you, Laura. I'm here to help."

A cautious relief flowed over her as she sat straight and tall on the seat, her auburn hair tumbling from its ponytail, soft wisps falling around her pale face. "I appreciate what you did tonight. You can drop me at the closest convenience store and I'll call someone to come and pick me up."

He grinned, having already summed up her type from shadowing her over the past two days. No gushy gratitude from this lady. She was set and determined to take care of herself. He admired that. She was a strong woman, but even strong women sometimes needed help. "Who?"

"Excuse me?"

"Who are you going to call to come get you?"

Her eyes widened as if surprised that he would ask and she took on an indignant tone. "I don't see how that's your business."

"I just rescued you from kidnappers. I'd hate to have wasted my time only to have them find you now."

A flush of anger crept over her face at his unwillingness to stop. "I appreciate your stepping in tonight, but I must insist you stop the truck and let me out. *Now.*"

He understood her frustration, but he also wasn't going to allow her to walk right back into a dangerous situation. "I'm afraid I can't do that, Laura."

"Again…how do you know my name?"

"I know all about you. My name is Colton Blackwell, in case you're interested."

"Thank you, I'm very interested. Now I know who to tell the police abducted me."

He flashed another grin, enjoying her quick wit. She was smart. He liked that. "You're not my prisoner."

"Then stop the truck and let me go."

"Think of this less as an abduction and more like protective custody."

"Are you a cop?" she asked.

"Nope. I'm a cattle farmer."

"A cattle farmer? *Really?* So a cattle farmer has kidnapped me and placed me in protective custody?"

He nodded grimly. "I'd say that's a fair assessment of what's happening."

She pulled her cell phone from the pocket of her scrub top. "I'm calling the police."

He couldn't allow that, either. He snatched the phone from her hand and tossed it out the open window.

"Hey, that's my phone!"

"They can use that to track you. Better safe than sorry," he said, keeping his eyes trained on the road. "I'm taking you to my ranch in Compton. It's about an hour's drive. My buddy is the sheriff there. I'll have him meet us and you can explain to him what happened."

She reluctantly sat back in the seat and her manner softened. "Look, *Colton*, I appreciate what you're trying to do, but what good can a small-town sheriff in Compton do? No one can help me."

"I trust him. He'll be able to help."

"This is not your problem. It's mine."

Her knew her story and saw the truth on her beautiful but sad face. It was a heavy burden she was carrying.

But she no longer had to shoulder it alone.

The hum of the highway and the soft sound of country music spilling from the radio greeted Laura as she awoke. The cab of the truck was dark except for the lights of the dash. She rubbed sleep from her eyes, surprised that she'd nodded off so easily. She shouldn't be surprised. She hadn't slept well in more than two weeks, not since she'd discovered the predicament her father had placed her in. She'd found herself triple-checking the doors of her apartment and even then sleeping fitfully in case someone tried to break in. But tonight, in the cab of Colton Blackwell's pickup truck, she'd slept soundly.

She stared at the black road stretching out in front of them, lit only by the bright lights of the truck. "Where are we?"

"About twenty minutes from my ranch in Compton, Louisiana."

She took a good long look at the man who had been her rescuer tonight. His face was sharp and angled and the stubble on his face appeared as rough-and-tumble as he seemed to be.

She turned away her eyes. She shouldn't be examining any part of this cattle rancher except his intentions toward her. "Why were you following me?"

"I heard you were in trouble. Whenever I hear of someone in trouble, I try to help if I can."

"What makes you think you can help me?"

"It's kind of what I do, Laura. I used to be an army ranger. When I got out of the service, I looked around for something else I would be good at. This is where my skills lie, so I try to lend a hand if I hear of someone in trouble. Think of me as your very own private security."

"But how did you know I was in trouble? Who told you about me?"

"Your father told me about your predicament. He was worried someone might be after you. It looks like he was right to be worried."

"My father hired you? I don't think so. He doesn't have any money. He can't afford to pay you."

"I didn't ask for anyone to pay me." He shrugged. "I only want to continue to protect and serve."

She sat, tense, uncertain what to do. On the one hand, Colton had saved her from a kidnapping. Those men had undoubtedly belonged to Randall. In his last communication with her, he'd told her he was tired of waiting. But on the other hand, Colton was a stranger and just another man making assurances to her he might not keep. How could she trust him?

He turned off the road and Laura saw a two-story ranch house appear in the headlights. As they approached, she glimpsed a barn off to one side and a large metal shop to the other side. He parked in front of the house and cut the engine.

"I know you don't know me, but I really do just want to help keep you safe, Laura. This isn't my first time involved in something like this, and I'm good at what I do. You'll be protected here, I promise. I won't let anything happen to you."

She glanced around at the house and barn. No one else appeared to be around. There were no other cars in the driveway and no lights on inside the house, but she did hear the sound of dogs barking in the distance. They were all alone out here together. If circumstances were different, she knew she could be in real trouble. She was reminded of one of those movies that claimed that no one would hear you scream.

Still, she couldn't be too careful. "I want to call my father."

"I don't think that's a good idea. No one knows you're here and I'd like to keep it that way. That means you don't call friends, family or coworkers. Those men will keep searching for you. Don't make it easy for them to track you down." He slid from the truck and walked around to open her door.

Laura slid from the truck and let him lead her toward the house. Everything he said made sense, but his words had dual meaning. If no one knew where she was, then no one would know what had happened to her if Colton Blackwell turned out to not be what he seemed.

He flipped on light switches as he entered the house, illuminating simple yet comfortable furnishings. It wasn't fancy, but Laura wasn't used to fancy.

"Do you live alone?"

"Yes. I bought this place two years ago, after I left the service."

She spotted a photograph on the mantel of Colton

with a group of men all in uniform. "You said you were a ranger. Was this your unit?"

He nodded, but a terse look crossed his face. "It was."

She saw his pained expression before he pushed it away. She recognized that look. She'd seen it many times during her stint as a nurse in the ER. It was the look of someone whose loved one had passed away. She'd heard about the Army Rangers and knew the work they did was dangerous. He'd lost men, probably one or more of the men in the photograph, and probably in battle.

"The one on the end is Blake Michaels. He's the deputy sheriff I told you about." Colton started for the staircase. "I'll show you where you can sleep."

He opened a door at the top of the stairs and Laura looked around at the simple bed, dresser and chair. It wasn't fancy, but it was cozy and clean. She glanced at the dresser drawers and realized she had nothing to put inside them. She hadn't had time to pack a bag and her extra scrubs were in her backpack, which she assumed was now lying abandoned in the hospital's employee parking lot.

"You'll have your own private bathroom," Colton continued, motioning toward a closed door. "There should be some extra toothbrushes in the cabinet and we'll go into town tomorrow to buy whatever else you think you might need."

He kept extra toothbrushes? That meant this wasn't the first time he'd intervened to help someone. It seemed to confirm what he'd told her in the truck. "I take it I'm not the first person you've helped to stay in this room."

He stared at her, his brown eyes filled with dismay. "You don't trust much, do you?"

His words were true if unwelcome. "I've never had much reason to trust easily."

"Well, you can trust me, Laura."

She wanted to believe that, but she'd been burned too many times before.

"I've already moved my stuff downstairs. I'll be sleeping on the couch while you're here, so you'll have the entire upstairs. If you need anything, holler."

After he left, Laura locked the bedroom door. She glanced around at the room. This was her safe haven for now. No one knew where she was or what had happened to her. A phone sat on the end table and she considered phoning her father to let him know she was safe, but she decided against it. Would her father worry about her? A part of her was happy to think that he might spend a few restless nights fretting about her. Or would he simply assume she'd taken care of his debt? No, Colton had said her father had been the one to hire him. He was trying to fix the mess he'd gotten her into.

It was small consolation.

She shuddered at the thought of what might have happened to her if Colton Blackwell hadn't been there. And, despite the fact that she didn't know if she could really trust him, she was thankful for his help.

Colton headed downstairs. He felt better having Laura under his roof. If anyone was coming after her, they would have to face him on his own turf.

He hated how distrustful she seemed, unwilling to

believe that anyone would want to help her without
asking for something in return. She was clearly so
used to being disappointed that she couldn't imagine
things going any other way.

*God, please help her to believe that I only want to
protect her. And grant me the strength and discernment
to keep her safe from harm.*

He pulled out his phone and dialed Bill Jackson's
number, his stomach turning as he made the call. This
was the man who had caused Laura so much pain and
grief. It was too real seeing the pain in her face. He
knew that look. Oh, how well he knew that look.

"It's me," he said when Bill answered. "I have her.
She's safe."

He listened to the rush of thanks and gratitude from
the other end but soon cut him off. He hadn't intervened
for this man's sake, regardless of how thankful he was.
He'd done it for Laura and to make up in some way for
the mistakes he'd made. Laura Jackson represented to
him every person his own gambling addiction had hurt.
If he could keep her safe, maybe he could make up for
his past, even if just a little.

Laura's mind raced. Sleep was impossible. Thoughts
of the night's events kept playing over and over again,
reminding her that she was in a stranger's home. How
had she just gotten into the man's truck and driven
away with him? Away from everything and everyone
familiar to her? Yes, she'd been under attack. Those
men had been out to get her. But how did she know
Colton Blackwell wasn't one of Randall's men, as well?

For all she knew, his intervention had been planned, premeditated, to get her right where Randall wanted her—alone, frightened, vulnerable…and looking for a hero.

She stopped that line of thinking before she made herself crazy. Randall's men had been after her and Colton had rescued her. She'd acted on instinct, going along with him because she'd had no choice. But that didn't mean she had to remain with him now that the moment of danger had passed.

She picked up the phone to call for help, then realized she had no idea where she was…except for the city. Compton. That was, of course, assuming he'd been telling her the truth. She couldn't trust him. After all, the only thing she knew about Colton Blackwell was that he'd said he had been watching her. What if he was worse than Randall? There was no telling what this man wanted from her.

Certainly she'd been acting purely on adrenaline before. But now that she'd had plenty of time to digest what was happening, she realized she had to get away from him. Now. Tonight. She would sneak out and flag down a car for help.

She slipped back into her shoes and quietly unlocked the bedroom door. Opening it softly, she walked to the top of the stairs and peeked down. The house looked dark except for the dim light above the kitchen range. She glanced at the sofa bed where Colton said he would be sleeping and saw a figure wrapped in a blanket. Now was her time to escape—while he was asleep. Hopefully she would be well out of his grasp before he awakened in the morning.

She tiptoed across the floor and quietly pulled open the door.

"Don't move!" Colton hollered, leaping from the sofa bed and pointing a gun at her.

"Please don't hurt me," Laura cried out. Her heart raced with fear at the sight of Colton's gun trained on her. This only confirmed what she'd been afraid of: Colton Blackwell was not her friend.

He flipped on the light and the intensity of his expression fell. "Laura, I nearly shot you." Lowering the gun, he rasped, "What are you *doing*?"

She pressed herself against the door and tried to breathe. No telling what he might do to her now that he'd caught her trying to sneak away. Would he continue with the charade of trying to protect her? She struggled to find her voice against the rapid shaking of her muscles. "Please, just let me go. I won't tell anyone who you are." Tears streamed down her face. "Please. I just want to go home."

His expression softened and he nodded. "Okay, Laura. Okay." He placed the gun on the table and then turned to her. "I'm not going to hurt you. I only want to help you."

But all the reasons why she couldn't trust him kept flittering through her mind. She didn't know him. She didn't know his intentions. How could she really believe him? And why would someone like him want to help someone like her?

He gave a resigned sigh. "Let's try this another way."

He grabbed the truck keys from the end table and held them out to her. "Take these. Take the truck. Take my phone. Call your father and confirm my story, but don't tell him where you are. If he knows, Randall could force him to tell." He pulled cash from his wallet. "Take this money. Find a hotel and hole up there for a few days. But don't go home, Laura. You're not safe at home."

The keys shook in her hand. "You...you're letting me go?"

"You're not my prisoner. If you don't want my protection, fine. I get it. You don't know me. If this is the only way you'll allow me to help you, then take it."

She turned and ran to the truck, certain he would be right behind her to stop her, certain this was all a sick trick to make her trust him. But he was offering her a way out and she was going to take it.

She climbed into the truck and started the engine. Colton was still on the porch, standing, watching her, making no move to stop her. She jammed the truck into gear and sped up the drive. She saw him in the mirror, still watching, making no move to stop her or to follow her.

She stopped at the end of the drive. The house was no longer visible and the darkness of the road stretched in front of her. She had no idea where she was going or what she was going to do. Her pulse was slowing; fear of the unknown replacing her need to flee. If she left Colton, she had no idea what she was getting into. Randall and his men were still coming for her, and if they'd tried to abduct her once, they would do it again.

She leaned against the steering wheel as confusion

confounded her. Was it really possible that Colton was just who he'd said he was and that all he wanted was to help her? All she knew for certain was that bad men were after her and that Colton had done nothing but protect her from them.

She glanced at his cell phone on the seat beside her. Colton had said her father had hired him and that would be easy enough to confirm. She picked up his phone and recognized her dad's number listed under his recent calls.

She pressed the number and waited. He answered on the third ring.

"Dad, something happened tonight."

"I know, Laura. Colton already called me. Are you okay, honey?"

"I—I don't know. Who is this guy, Dad? How do I know I can trust him?"

There was a long pause. "You can trust him, Laura. I believe he really wants to help."

"I can't believe this is happening," she snapped. "I can't believe you did this to me."

She heard the catch in his voice as he rushed to apologize. "Laura, I'm sorry. I never thought this would happen."

She caught herself before she said what she was really thinking. *You never thought about me, only about yourself.*

"Well, it's a little too late for regrets now, don't you think?"

"Laura, please, I—"

Satisfied that the army ranger had indeed been hired

by her father and unwilling to stomach any more of Bill Jackson's lame excuses, Laura clicked off the phone.

She needed to trust Colton Blackwell—and pray he was the good guy he appeared to be.

Taking a deep, bolstering breath, she put the truck into Reverse, turned around and headed back toward the house.

He was still on the porch, barefoot, his dark hair disheveled, as if he'd been running his hands through it. He'd obviously not made a move even to put his boots on. She pulled up to the porch and stopped the truck.

She stared at him through the open window, glad she'd returned, because no matter what her overly analytical mind said, she needed to trust this man with her life.

She was shivering when Colton led her into the house. He doubted it was from the slight breeze in the night air, though, as much as the threats against her. He ushered her into the kitchen and pulled out a chair. She sat watching him as he turned on the coffee and let it brew, then lowered his large, muscular frame into an adjacent chair and got down to business. "Let's talk about who is after you, Laura. Your father already gave me the basics, but I'd like to hear it from you. Who were those men tonight?"

Her chin quivered as the weight of her situation settled into her. "They work for a man named Chuck Randall."

"The loan shark?"

"You know him?"

Colton knew him well. He'd had dealings with him once or twice back in his gambling days. "I've heard of him. He prowls the casinos in River City looking for souls desperate enough to utilize his services. But what does he want with you?"

Her face reddened and she lowered her head, shame coloring her face. "My father is indebted to him."

"And he wants to use you as leverage to get your father to pay?"

"Not exactly. It started with him wanting me to cover my dad's bills. I refused, but he kept hassling me. He threatened me. He said my father would die if I didn't pay. Finally he said he would wipe out my father's debt if I did something for him."

"What does he want you to do, Laura?" Colton asked, his face already grim in anticipation of her response.

A sob caught in her throat and her calm began to unravel. Her hands shook and he could see voicing the truth was painful and bitter. "He wants me to marry him. And if I don't, he will kill my father."

Colton was stunned. This went beyond just getting payment for gambling debts. It had already escalated into something much more sinister. Money could be paid back, but if Randall had set his eyes on Laura and she'd rebuked him, she could be in real danger.

"I tried to tell him I wasn't interested, but his advances only got worse. He phoned me constantly. He sent me flowers and gifts. He even showed up at my work. I begged him to leave me alone. Why would he want someone who doesn't want him?"

Colton wasn't surprised. "Randall is used to getting whatever he wants. He's used to owning people through his money. It's about power. When he couldn't control you with money or threats or gifts, he became obsessed with having you. He sent men after you, which means either he's decided to take you by force or else he wants you to pay for what he would consider the ultimate betrayal."

She shuddered, rightly frightened by the situation she was in, and he had the sudden urge to take her into his arms and comfort her. He pushed back that feeling and instead steeled himself with determination to keep her safe from Randall and his crazy demands.

"How do I convince him to stop? I'll give him the money. I'll pay him whatever he wants to leave me alone."

"You can't, Laura. It's no longer about money. It's about control."

She shuddered again and he rushed to reassure her, placing his hand over hers and relishing the softness of her skin. "I told you, Laura, this is what I do, and I'm good at my job. Don't worry. We'll find you a way out of this mess."

She turned those wide green eyes full of hope on him. He'd seen situations like this before and knew they didn't often work out well, but he didn't let that sway his resolve. He would keep her safe no matter what it took.

"What about my father?"

"Randall will put pressure on him to uncover your whereabouts, but he can't tell what he doesn't know. Bill doesn't know where I live. I never even told him my last name. Did you call him?"

"Yes," she replied.

Narrowing his eyes, he gave her a look. "You didn't tell him where you are, did you?"

"No, I didn't tell him."

She shivered at the thought that Randall might hurt her dad just to get to her. A tear slipped from her eye. She wiped it away quickly. The last thing she wanted was for Colton to feel sorry for him.

"You're worried about him?" he asked gently.

She pushed away that worry and shook her head. She was done crying for him. "He brought this on me. He placed my life in danger so he could try for his next big score. He stopped thinking of me as a daughter a long time ago."

"Gambling is just like any other drug. It's a crutch—"

Laura stopped him before he continued. She was sure he meant well, but she'd heard it all before. "Spare me the 'gambling is an addiction' spiel, Colton. I can't tell you how many people have tried to tell me my dad has a sickness and that he can't help himself. I tried to help him. I tried everything I knew to do to help him, but he didn't want my help." Her anger rising, she blew out a frustrated breath. "All he wanted from me was another handout, and when I stopped giving them, he stopped coming around. I'm sorry for the hole he's dug himself into, but now he's dragged me into it with him, and if only one of us can get out of it, it's going to be me. I won't continue to let his problem control me."

She turned away from him, walked back into the den and plopped down on the couch, sinking into the cushions and hoping Colton wouldn't continue to try to justify her father's actions. She needed to stay mad at her dad. It was the only thing that was holding her together. But if Colton kept pulling at that string, her entire demeanor might unravel. She couldn't let that happen. She wouldn't do herself any good if she became a hysterical mess.

Colton obviously took the hint. "It's late and I realize you haven't had anything to eat since you got off work. Why don't I whip you up some eggs?"

She appreciated all he'd done for her, all he was trying to do for her, but there was no point in him cooking for her. She hadn't eaten since her lunch break, now nearly eight hours ago, but the pit in her stomach would prevent her from keeping anything down. "I appreciate the thought, but I'm just going to go upstairs and try to get some sleep."

He was by her side in an instant. "Laura, I'm sorry if I upset you." His handsome face was full of kindness and concern. For one crazy moment she imagined stepping into his embrace and weeping against his strong shoulders. But that was only a pipe dream.

"None of this is your fault, Colton. In fact, you're the one bright spot in all of this."

In fact, she didn't know what she would have done without him and his intervention. She should never have doubted him. She'd prayed for a way out of this mess, and God had sent her Colton. For that, she was grateful, although she would have preferred that God make the entire mess go away so she could continue on with her life.

Would she ever have a normal life again? She realized she'd taken normalcy for granted when she'd had it. When her mom had gotten sick and died, her father had turned to the casinos for comfort. Laura's life had not been the same since.

She longed for the assurance of a job where no one knew how dysfunctional her family was, and the stability of a home that didn't include having to sneak out in the middle of the night because her dad had gambled away the rent money. Mostly, she longed for a loving relationship. That one day she'd have someone who would stand beside her and share her burdens, and she could share his… A lump rose to her throat. But who would *ever* want to share the burdens she carried? Any man in his right mind would run screaming for the hills when he discovered her twisted family ties.

She swallowed hard, determined not to let her vulnerability show. For now, she had Colton, and she would take what she could get for as long as she could. Because eventually he would realize the depth of the hole her father had dug for her, and he would realize the futility of trying to help her out of it. He would be gone, just like the rest, because the load she carried was too heavy for anyone else to bear.

He stopped her before she reached the stairs. "Laura, we all make choices that have consequences. Some of those consequences are worse than others. I'm sure your father never meant to do anything to cause you harm."

"He's getting what he deserves. He brought this on, not me. I can't concern myself with him right now." She rushed up the stairs and locked herself in the bedroom before the tears began to fall.

* * *

Colton leaned against the sink. Laura might as well have punched him in the gut. It felt the same. Her words had hit him. Hard. She didn't know it, but she could have been talking about him when she'd spoken about her father. She was a living, breathing, in-your-face reminder of all the people he'd hurt through his dark time.

If she knew the truth about his past, she would turn tail and run as far from him as she could get…and then Chuck Randall would get to her.

But if Colton could rescue her, then maybe he could gain a bit of redemption, too.

TWO

Laura's eyes fluttered open. Sunlight filtered in through the curtain. She lifted up onto her elbows and glanced at the bedside clock. It was already afternoon. She'd slept most of the day and had to admit she felt rested for the first time in a long while.

She owed it to Colton and his presence. But even though she felt safe here, she knew she couldn't afford to let her guard down. She heard his voice from outside her window. Glancing out, she saw him walking toward the barn, several dogs following along behind him. She raised the window and heard him talking to them. It caused her to smile that he talked to his dogs. She liked that about him. Then her face reddened as she realized that wasn't all she liked about Colton. She enjoyed the way his shirt pulled tight against him, revealing broad shoulders and muscles for decades.

Transfixed, she watched him kneel and pet one of the dogs that jumped up on him, rubbing him affectionately. He suddenly glanced her way. She reddened again, this time at being caught staring. But he good-naturedly raised his hand in a wave to her.

She moved away from the window. Trusting Colton to keep her safe was one thing, but finding herself drawn to the man was another. Still, she couldn't deny the attraction. But then, why wouldn't she be affected? A good-looking man had swooped in and rescued her from the bad men. Her feelings were probably natural, but she couldn't act on them. She didn't have a great track record with men. Her last serious relationship had ended ugly, causing her to realize the idiom that girls fall in love with men like their fathers wasn't just a saying. It was true. Lance liked the casinos as much as her father did. Once she'd realized this, she'd quickly ended the relationship. She already had one gambler in her life and certainly didn't need another.

Before she went downstairs, she took a few moments to phone her neighbor Mrs. Duncan. Laura told her she was going to be out of town for a few days and asked her to check in on her cat, Misty, and to make sure she had food. Mrs. Duncan agreed and wished her a good trip. Laura hated not being honest with her, but she thought this was the best way. Colton hadn't even wanted her to phone, but she couldn't go into hiding while her kitty starved.

Next, she called her friend Denise Jenkins, another nurse in the ER. She wanted to let her know she was safe and ask her to pass along the message to the nurse manager that she'd had to go out of town unexpectedly, so they could remove her from the work schedule and find someone to cover her upcoming shifts.

Denise sounded groggy when she answered and

Laura remembered that her friend had worked the graveyard shift. She'd begun her shift while Laura was finishing hers. Laura glanced at the clock and realized her friend had probably just gotten home and into bed an hour or so ago.

"Denise, it's Laura. Are you awake?"

"I am now," she moaned. "Why are you calling me so early? You know I just got off work."

"I know. I wouldn't have called, but it's important. Something happened last night. A group of men tried to abduct me in the employee parking lot."

"What!" Denise's voice cleared and Laura could tell she was now fully alert. "Are you okay? Are you being held captive? Should I call the police?"

"No, no. I'm fine. Another man was there and he rescued me. I'm safe, but I don't think I'm going to be returning to River City for a while."

"Did you go to the police? Did they find the guys who tried to get you?"

"No, we didn't go to the police. You know this wasn't a random kidnapping attempt. Randall sent those men to grab me."

She had told Denise about her father's gambling debts and Randall's insistence she pay, but not the rest—the horrible truth that Randall was demanding she marry him. She shuddered, thinking about the idea of him ever laying a hand on her.

"Are you sure you're okay?" Denise asked her.

"Yes, for now. Anyway, the reason I called is that I didn't want you to worry about me, but I also need you to call the nurse manager and ask her to take me off the schedule. Just tell her I'll call when I get back into town."

"When will that be?" Denise asked, her voice growing ever more frightened.

"I don't know. Maybe not for a while. I don't have my phone anymore, so you can't call it, but you can reach me at this number."

Denise was silent on the other end for several moments. Laura wondered if she'd hung up or fallen back asleep, but when she spoke, Laura could hear the uncertainty and fear in her tone. "Laura, tell me the truth, is someone there with you now? Are they making you say this?"

"No, Denise. I'm fine. Will you please just do as I asked?"

"I will. I'll take care of it later this afternoon. And will you do me a favor? Stay safe."

"I will," Laura promised, then hung up the phone, not knowing if she would ever see her friend again.

By the time she dressed, Colton was on the front porch in one rocker, a mug of coffee in his hand. Laura spotted a well-worn leather Bible in his lap. He placed it aside as she stepped outside. The dogs lazing at his feet lifted their heads to her curiously.

"Afternoon. How'd you sleep?"

"Good. Too good. Why didn't you wake me sooner?"

"What for? I guessed you could use some catching up on your sleep. I made breakfast. Nothing fancy, just eggs and bacon. I saved you some."

"Thanks, but I'm not hungry." She sat in the opposite

rocker and one of the dogs—a brown mutt—moseyed over and sniffed around her. Laura held out her hand to him, then reached down and petted him.

"That's Milo." He pointed out the other dogs one by one. "This is Freddie, Rowdy and Miss Roxie."

Laura scratched behind Milo's ear. "How are you, boy?" In response, he jumped up onto her lap. "What kind of dog is he?"

"He's just a run-of-the-mill mutt. All of them are. No thoroughbreds here." He gave her a wry look. "I hope you like animals because I have a mess of them. The dogs are good for alerting when someone is approaching the house."

"I heard them last night, but I didn't see them."

"I had them penned up."

"I love animals," she confided. "I have a cat. Misty. When I was younger, I always dreamed of becoming a veterinarian."

His eyes alight with interest, he asked curiously, "What happened to that dream?"

She sighed. As with most other things, her father's gambling had stolen another dream from her. "Life happened."

He must have sensed her reluctance to talk about it because he set aside his Bible as he stood.

"I thought we would go into town and see about getting you some clothes and such. But first I want to give you the layout of the ranch." He walked to the front door and she saw a small box mounted on the wall. "I always keep the alarm set. The passcode is 824. It's set to ring to my cell phone if it's set off. I also wanted to show you this." He moved through the house to the kitchen and into the laundry room, but it wasn't just any laundry room. He pushed open a closet to reveal what appeared to be a weapons arsenal.

He reached for a handgun. "Have you ever fired a gun?"

"No." She knew many men in this part of the country hunted, but her father had never been one of them. Guns cost money and he'd preferred spending that money at the casinos.

Laura stared at the incredible display of weapons, some small handguns and some larger. She didn't know much about weapons, but she knew not all he had were for recreational use. "Do you really know how to shoot all of these?"

"Each and every one. I wouldn't have them if I didn't know how to handle them."

He set the handgun back into its place and closed the door. "You should know, too, that I almost always have a gun on me." He opened his jacket to reveal a gun and holster. "The Rangers are an infiltration group. It was our job to go into an area and clear it of enemy risks. It was a dangerous job, but we got it done and it taught me to never be afraid. Fear of the unknown is often your worst enemy when you're doing battle."

She stared up into his handsome, now clean-shaven face. It seemed to her that he must not fear anything or anyone. He'd swooped in to save her, staring down the barrel of a gun just to protect someone he didn't even know.

She suddenly felt a rush of gratitude wash over her.

So much for keeping a level head around him. She stared up at him. "Thank you for helping me, Colton. I don't know what would have happened to me if you hadn't shown up when you did." Tears pricked behind her eyelids, but she willed them away, not wanting to appear weak in front of him.

He bent and locked gazes with her, his warm, brown eyes assuring her it was okay to be scared. "I will keep you safe, Laura," he told her. "I promise I will keep you safe."

How long had it been since she'd been able to trust a man, any man?

She wanted so badly to believe in this one.

Laura had fled River City with only the clothes she'd been wearing from her shift at the hospital. He'd loaned her one of his T-shirts to sleep in while she'd washed and dried her scrubs and she was stuck wearing them again today. But women needed things besides clothes, so they were off to town. Compton didn't have big-name shops or fancy restaurants, but the town had the essentials.

As they drove, Colton tried to reassure Laura that finding the ranch would be difficult for anyone who didn't know where they were. They'd come in last night when it was dark, so she hadn't noticed the acres of land surrounding them. "We don't have a lot of traffic on this road anymore, so I don't have many close neighbors," he said.

In fact, his closest neighbor had recently moved away. She was an elderly widow who had run a drive-in movie theater with her husband back when the highway was a main thoroughfare. Once the interstate rerouted traffic from the highway, the drive-in had faltered and eventually closed. However, the widow had lived on the grounds until she'd moved to live with her daughter. The screen was in disrepair but still standing in the middle of a field, which he thought was cool.

He drove to a large retail store off the interstate that was central to three adjoining towns. If anyone saw them that he didn't know, they would still have a difficult time pinpointing where Laura was staying.

To his surprise, Colton ran into someone he knew soon after they entered the store. He heard his name being called, then looked up to see Miranda Ryan heading their way. She was pushing a buggy loaded with groceries. Miranda was engaged to his friend and former army ranger friend Blake. "Miranda, hi."

"Colton, I'm glad to see you." She gave him a hug, then glanced curiously at Laura. "Who is your friend?"

"Miranda, this is Laura Jackson. I'm working a protection detail for her."

"It's nice to meet you," Laura said graciously.

"You, too," Miranda responded. She was obviously intrigued about seeing Colton with an unknown woman, but she didn't question him about her. "Blake has been trying to call you for days. He's nearly ready to send the Rangers out looking for you."

He knew what that meant. He was worried about where he was and what he was doing. "I'm okay. I'll call him."

"Good." She started to push her buggy away, then stopped and gave Colton a knowing wink. "She's cute."

"It's not like that, Miranda."

She didn't seem convinced. "Whatever you say, Colton." She turned to Laura. "It was nice to meet you."

"You, too."

He envied what his friend Blake had with Miranda.

Compton had become a safe haven for Colton since leaving the Rangers. The quiet, laid-back lifestyle suited his needs. He had nearly everything he needed here, except someone to share it with. He was ready to settle down and start a family, and had been thinking about it more and more lately. But he doubted that would even be possible given his past.

He watched as Laura sorted through clothes on the rack. She was just the kind of woman he would choose to fall for if he could. She was beautiful and smart, and she was compassionate, too. He'd seen it when he'd trailed her, noticing her kindness toward her elderly neighbor. Even the way she'd bent and rubbed his old mutt this morning on the porch had touched his soul. Laura was a good person, a giver. And too many people had already taken more from her than she had to give.

She tucked her hair behind her ear as she leaned over the rack to get a closer look at the tag. He got an up close view of her creamy white skin and long, graceful neck. She moved her head and caught him staring, but she didn't look upset. Instead her pink lips lifted at the corners, then she turned back to the jeans's tag.

He pulled his eyes away from her and tried to focus

on something else. No sense pining after something he could never have.

He spotted a man looking their way and Colton's radar went off. It was possible he was merely admiring Laura's good looks. She was a fresh, new face in town, after all. But something about the man's expression caught Colton's attention. The man kept glancing at his phone, then curiously back at Laura.

He was probably overreacting. No one knew Laura was here. No one could know. Still, he led her away from that department and headed for the grocery aisle with the excuse that he needed to pick up a few things. She went willingly and didn't argue.

As they approached the frozen foods section, Colton spotted the man again. This time he was peeking out from behind a freezer, his cell phone raised as if he were trying to get a photo of them.

"Wait right here," Colton told her. He moved away from her and around the freezers. The man's eyes never left Laura, further confirming for Colton that he was targeting her. He approached the man from behind, grabbed him by the shirt and yanked his phone from his hand.

"Hey, what are you doing?" the man protested.

Anger pulsed through him when he scanned the device and saw several photos of Laura on the man's phone. "Why are you watching her?"

"I—I need the money. At first I thought it was nothing, but then when I saw her, I couldn't believe it. I'm in deep. I need the money."

"What are you talking about? What money?"

"The reward." He motioned toward the cell phone. "It was posted this morning on one of the social media sites I'm on. I, of course, just scrolled on through it, but when I saw her…"

"Show me," Colton demanded, then watched eagle-eyed as the man scrolled through his social media pages. He stopped when he found what he was searching for and showed it to Colton. "Here it is. Like I said, I couldn't believe it was her."

The image stopped his blood cold—a photo of Laura with the caption Have You Seen This Woman? There was a reward for anyone who could bring her home.

The message had been posted this morning by an account named Bring Laura Home. Colton saw that it had already been liked and shared many times.

Colton noted that the man hadn't yet given away Laura's location…and he wouldn't.

He pocketed the phone. "You'll forget about her if you know what's good for you. Bother her again and I'll make sure you regret it. Got it?"

The man nodded solemnly. He didn't seem like a threat, just an opportunist, and that was what Randall had been hoping for by sending out that message.

He'd in essence placed a bounty on Laura's head and Colton was sure there would be a line of people hoping to collect.

He sent the man on his way, then retrieved Laura. "We have to leave now."

He grabbed her arm and led her away.

"Wait! What about the buggy?"

"Leave it," he barked, hurrying her along.

Anger bit through him at his own foolishness. He'd let down his guard and placed Laura in a perilous situation. Protecting her should have been his first priority.

"What's going on?" she asked in a low voice as they made it to the truck. "What happened back there?"

Fear tinged her features, making him feel like a heel for getting so worked up.

"It was probably nothing, but I'd rather not take the chance."

She crawled into the truck. Colton scanned the parking lot and the front of the store, making certain the mystery man hadn't followed them out. Satisfied he hadn't, Colton slid into the truck, gunned the engine and roared away before anyone had the opportunity to follow.

Whatever had happened at the store had Colton shaken. She could see it in his tense muscles and the vein throbbing in his neck as he drove like a maniac. He didn't let up on the accelerator until he pulled into the ranch and stopped the truck in front of the house.

"What happened back there?" Laura asked him again as they got out of the truck and walked inside.

He locked the door, then turned to her. "Someone was watching you." He pulled a cell phone from his pocket and handed it to her. "He had this on him."

She opened the phone and saw a message on the screen asking for information about her location and offering a reward. She gasped at the amount. Ten thousand dollars was a lot of money, but she supposed that was only a drop in the bucket, since her father still owed Randall close to fifty thousand dollars.

"It looks like Randall is reaching out to anyone who might know your whereabouts."

"This man had my picture and he was watching us." She swallowed hard. "Did he follow us there?"

"I don't think so. I think he just happened upon us and recognized you from your photo."

Her heart started pounding and fear crept into her soul again. It seemed Randall would do anything to get his hands on her.

"I thought you said I was safe, that no one knew I was here."

"No one does and no one is going to know," he rushed to assure her. "We just need to stay low here at the ranch and not go out in public again."

"But he knows. This man knows I'm here."

"He only knows approximately. That store is ten miles away from here and there's a lot of country between there and here. Besides, it's centrally located. For all he knows, we could be in another city. We're still okay." He turned away, heading for the kitchen.

She stared at the phone number at the bottom of the message. It was most assuredly Randall's number. She recognized it from the multiple calls he'd placed to her trying to win her affection.

Laura thought about the men last night. She'd seen their expressions in the lamplight. They'd been on a mission and she was their target. Had Colton not been there, she didn't know what might have happened to her.

Without a second thought, she dialed the number. It rang twice before a man answered.

"It's Laura," she said through clenched teeth. "I'm calling to tell you to leave me alone."

"Laura! Where are you? I've been searching all over for you."

"I know you have. I'm calling to tell you to stop hounding me. Don't you understand I don't want anything to do with you?"

"I'm afraid that's not possible, Laura. You belong to me now and no one is going to keep us apart...not even that loser cowboy you've taken off with. My men told me all about him swooping in and whisking you away. I will find out who he is and then I will find you and, when I do, you'll have a lot of explaining to do." The threat in his voice was real and terrifying.

"Who are you talking to?" Colton asked, reappearing in the den.

Laura was at a loss for words even as Randall ranted on in her ear. "Is that him? Tell him I'm coming for him, Laura. I will find you and, when I do, you'll be sorry you left me."

Colton grabbed the phone from her and listened a moment as Randall's threats continued. The last words she heard before Colton threw down the phone and smashed it with the heel of his boot was Randall's promise to butcher them both if she didn't return home.

She stared up at Colton warily as common sense prevailed. "I don't know why I called him." She hardly even remembered dialing the phone. All she knew now was that it had been useless, pointless. Randall controlled her life now more than ever. Even when she wasn't with him, she was thinking about him and wondering if and when he would find her. She hated the feeling of loss of control that he'd saddled her with. It wasn't fair that a man she hardly knew could have so much power over her life.

Colton sat beside her on the couch. She expected him to be angry at her foolishness, but instead she saw understanding in his expression. "You needed to try one more time."

She nodded. He did understand. "There should be something I can do, something I can say, that will end all of this and make him just leave me alone."

"There isn't," Colton said grimly.

Well, she wouldn't continue to be Randall's victim. But she also didn't want to depend on someone else to keep her safe. "I want you to do something for me, Colton. I want you to teach me to shoot a gun. I want to be able to protect myself if I need to."

He didn't seem surprised by her request. He only nodded and said, "Okay."

Laura stared at the smashed phone on the floor, imagined that was Randall's head and kicked it herself.

She wouldn't be his victim any longer.

Teaching Laura how to shoot was an excellent idea and he was glad she was up for it. He loaded up an ATV with weapons and a few rounds. It felt good to be doing something, anything, besides sitting around and waiting. His lips quirked as he watched Laura walk out of the house wearing one of his T-shirts tied at the waist, her pretty auburn hair floating in the breeze. Milo tromped along behind her as she approached him. The dog had taken a quick liking to her and he couldn't blame him. She just kept growing in his estimation. And her spunk and determination truly amazed him. When he'd realized she'd called Randall and confronted him again, he'd been terrified at first and then proud that she was still able to stand up for herself after all the man had put her through.

"Are we going somewhere?" she asked when she noticed the ATV.

"I thought we'd go out onto the edge of the pasture so the gunfire doesn't spook the animals."

He hopped onto the ATV and she climbed on behind him, wrapping her arms around his waist. He was mega aware of the daintiness of them as he started the engine and set out across the pasture.

He still couldn't believe Randall was demanding she marry him. It sounded to him like something that would happen in the Third World countries he'd been in, not in modern-day America. It was a terrible situation for anyone to find themselves in. But the bitter taste in his mouth was so familiar. The fact that her father's gambling had pulled her into this mess resonated with him. He was constantly amazed at how far people would go—how far he'd gone—in the name of the next big score.

He didn't like remembering how far he'd fallen before his ranger brothers had intervened for him. But, besides him, who else would intervene on behalf of Laura?

He reached the clearing and set up a target of aluminum cans. He then ran through a basic tutorial on the pistol he'd picked out for her.

"Are you sure you're up for this?" he asked gruffly.

"Absolutely."

He held out the weapon to her. "It's heavier than it looks." When he gave her the full weight, her eyes widened.

She raised the gun, aiming it toward the cans. Colton stood behind her, reaching around her to move her hands into the correct positions. He noted the way her body fit just right between his arms. The scent of her shampoo wafted up to his nostrils, sending his senses reeling. He had to push thoughts of her that had nothing to do with protecting her from his mind. His past was everything she'd been fighting against for years. He tried to concentrate on the task at hand.

"Be ready for a kickback. It can be jolting if you aren't used to it."

She fired the gun and it kicked, jarring her backward against his chest.

She squealed at the kick, then laughed. He grinned, understanding the rush she was feeling. The first time shooting a gun was a frightening yet exhilarating experience. To him, it had become second nature, so it had been a long time since he'd shared that feeling with anyone.

"That was amazing," she told him.

"Let's try it again."

She was a quick learner and soon became accustomed to the kick of the gun and even managed to hit one of the cans. With practice, he felt certain she could become an excellent marksman.

"You did good," he told her.

"Thank you for teaching me this. It helps. I feel a little bit more in control than I have. I keep asking myself how this all happened to me. I should have been able to do something or say something that would have prevented this."

"I doubt anything you could have done would have made much of a difference. Randall is dangerous."

Narrowing her eyes, she shot him a quizzical look. "How do you know about him?"

Personal experience. "I know the type," he said instead. "Driven, power-hungry, controlling."

"He doesn't seem to care that I want nothing to do with him."

"No, that probably makes him want you even more. It's the challenge, Laura. If he can take what he wants, it gives him a feeling of control."

She shook her head. "I can't believe my father put me in this position."

"How long has he been gambling?"

"My mother got sick when I was twelve. It started then. When she died, it was like the problem kicked into overdrive. He stopped going to work. He started taking the rent money, then the grocery money, then—" Her voice caught. "Somehow, I still don't know how he did it, but when I started college, my father managed to get into my bank account and take the money I'd saved for my tuition. He wiped me out. My tuition check bounced and I was politely asked to leave, since, according to their records, I was never truly enrolled."

His stomach turned at such a story of desperation. He remembered that feeling all too well, and it was just one more reminder of all the people he'd hurt. "Yet you kept going. You became a nurse."

"I worked nights, weekends, whatever I had to do to pay for my classes. I knew if I gave up, I'd be stuck forever. But it looks like I'm stuck regardless." Bitterness tinged her words.

It stung him. Being around Laura was a constant, painful reminder of all those he'd hurt. God had been reminding him about that lately, forcing him to come to terms with his behavior. But having her around was… hard. Real hard. She was clearly suffering, yet during times like these he felt powerless to help. All he knew to tell her was what God was teaching him about his own situation. "Forgiveness is the toughest thing of all, but usually it's the only thing that will set you free."

"Forgiveness?" She scoffed. "In the past several years, I've lost my mother, my father for all purposes and my future. He doesn't deserve my forgiveness."

They were the words he'd expected—still expected—to have thrown at him for his behavior, but his friends and family had been kind even though he was certain they must have harbored the same anger and resentment that Laura felt. His one gratitude was that at least he hadn't been married, hadn't become a father or a provider who'd failed those completely dependent on him. "Forgiveness isn't about what someone deserves. In fact, it's not even usually for the person that needs forgiving. I know I certainly didn't deserve forgiveness, but Jesus gave it regardless."

She stared at him. "I suppose you have to believe that to be a soldier. But you have no idea what I've been through. My father doesn't deserve the kind of absolution you're talking about."

"Sometimes, forgiveness is more for us than the other person. It releases us from the burden we carry around. At least, that was how it was for me."

She stared at him. "Who did you have to forgive?"

Something caught his ear before he could answer her. He glanced into the surrounding wooded area on the edge of the pasture. He'd definitely heard something moving in the brush. He gripped his gun and scanned the area. Probably it was just a deer or other critter, but it raised his senses regardless.

"Stay here," Colton told her as he moved toward where he'd heard the noise. He could discern nothing now, but he hadn't imagined it. Someone or something was out there and his instincts were on high alert.

He stopped and turned back to Laura. "Let's head back to the house."

She didn't argue as they moved to the ATV.

A shot rang out before they could climb on and leave. Colton felt something zing past him and jumped behind the ATV, pulling Laura down with him. He caught movement in the woods and then another round of shots rang out. His first instinct was to rush into the woods after the assailant, but his training kicked in. He couldn't leave Laura alone.

He glanced at her for the first time and realized how

pale she'd grown. She was holding her arm and blood was pooling around her shirtsleeve. Alarm skittered through him. "You were hit." He kicked himself for not noticing before he'd grabbed her arm and pulled her off her feet. She must be in terrible pain, yet she hadn't even cried out.

"It's nothing," she insisted. "Just a scratch. I just need to keep pressure on it."

He knew she was downplaying her injury. The way it was bleeding, it had to be more than a scratch. He pushed up her sleeve and saw that the bullet had clipped her shoulder, though it didn't look as if it had gone through. Still, it was bleeding like crazy.

"We have to get you back to the house."

But the shooter was still out there.

"When I say go, I want you to run into the woods. We'll have better cover there."

She nodded and he wondered if she had the strength. But he had to get her to cover.

He raised his gun. "Run!" he shouted, covering them by firing into the wooded area where the original shots had come from. He followed behind Laura as she sprinted across the grass and didn't relax until he heard the crunch of her feet against the brush. Even then, he didn't fully relax because the shooter was still out there, but now they were on even playing fields, which made him feel a smidgen better.

"Stay here," he whispered, parking her beside a tree while he went after the shooter. When she nodded, he moved quietly in the direction of the shots. A few yards away, he heard movement in the woods and spotted a fleeing figure dressed in camouflage.

"Freeze!" Colton yelled, running in that direction.

The camo-clad figure hopped onto a waiting motorcycle and took off.

Colton fired several shots, but the shooter roared away.

He didn't follow. Instead he hurried back to Laura, who had grown even paler. "Let's get back to the house."

They ran to the ATV and he asked, "Can you hold on to me?"

She grimaced, then shook her head. "I don't think so."

He helped her onto the front of the seat and then settled in behind her. She leaned back against him. The scent of her hair rushed through him as he started the ATV and took off across the pasture, going as gently as he could. She groaned in pain as the bumps jarred her, her face growing even paler. Her shirt was wet with blood and she felt frail in his arms.

Colton pushed forward, refocusing his attention on reaching the house.

How had he let this happen? He'd promised to protect her. He'd promised she was safe here, and he'd already let her down.

The wound wasn't nearly as serious as Colton was making it out to be. It hurt, but once they stopped the bleeding, it wouldn't be a life-threatening injury. He took the bumps through the pasture with ease, but she felt him cringe with each and every jolt. She tried not to cry out in pain, taking comfort in the strength of his arm cradling her as he maneuvered with his other hand. He was quickly becoming someone she felt she could depend on.

He stopped in front of the house and helped her to her feet, a rush of dizziness washing over her. Colton caught her before she fell, and the next thing she knew, she was swept up in his big, strong arms. He carried her inside and placed her gently on the couch.

"I'll get the first-aid kit," he said, rushing upstairs.

Laura did her best to sit up, leaning against the back of the couch. She pulled at her sleeve, now wet and sticky with blood. Colton returned and stripped the sleeve away, then cleaned the wound.

"How does it look?" she asked.

"It's a clean wound." She felt his pulse begin to calm. "Looks like it just grazed you."

"I'm fine," she insisted. "I don't need all this fuss."

"Let me fuss, Laura. I promised to protect you and I didn't. I underestimated Randall. That's a mistake I won't make again." She felt him shut down, pulling away from her emotionally as he bandaged her wound. It was evident from the tense set of his jaw that he was beating himself up as he worked through how this could have happened.

Her own tinge of guilt washed over her. She knew instinctively this was her fault. Had she inadvertently given away her location? "It was me, wasn't it? When I called Randall? I led him here."

He shook his head. "No, he wouldn't have had the time to do that before I crushed that phone. But from now on, you stay inside the house. No wandering around. I'll also start doing sweeps around the property. You'll be safe. I promise."

She saw worry crease his face. It reassured her in a strange way. She knew he took her safety seriously and *personally*. Was it possible this was a man she could trust to keep his word? She hoped so, because despite today's turn of events, she felt safe here with Colton. She found herself trusting that he would protect her.

THREE

Colton opened his weapons closet and double-checked his supplies. He'd let his guard down, lost his focus, and Randall had found a way to get to Laura. The pained look on her face as she napped on the couch was all the reminder he needed that he'd already failed her. He'd promised to protect her, assured her he was good at his job, then lost his focus at the sight of her.

He couldn't deny she was beautiful, and she wasn't the first pretty lady he'd protected without getting emotionally involved. But Laura was different. She was someone he knew he could never have. She'd said herself she was stuck because of her father's addiction. He could never ask her to take on his own past, as well. That wouldn't be fair to her.

He phoned Blake. He needed to bounce ideas off someone while Laura dozed on the couch.

Blake sounded exasperated when he answered. "I've been trying to reach you for days. Where have you been and why haven't you been answering my calls? I was worried about you, Colt. I nearly called in the Rangers until Miranda said she saw you at the store today."

Colton knew he was referring to his ranger brothers. They'd intervened before when Colton had hit rock bottom. "I'm fine. Really. You don't have to worry."

Blake sighed. "I'm glad you called finally. What's happening? Miranda said you had a woman with you?"

"I'm working a protection job that's gone bad. The man who's after my client is both powerful and obsessed with her. He's a loan shark in River City named Chuck Randall."

"You said it went bad. What happened?"

"Someone was here on my property. We were out by the back field and someone shot at us."

"Did you catch him?"

"No, he got away on a motorcycle before I could reach him. I had to get Laura to safety first."

"So you think this Randall followed you from River City?" his friend asked.

"No, he's not the type of person to do his own dirty work. He has her face plastered on social media and is offering a reward for her return. There was a man this morning at the store who was watching her." He cleared his throat, then went on. "I don't think he followed us back to the ranch, but maybe he recognized me and knew where I lived."

"You're sure no one followed you from River City? How careful were you?"

"I was careful, but…" He grimaced. In his old life he'd spent a fair amount of time in that city hitting the casinos and becoming familiar with the locals.

Blake obviously saw the direction he was headed and

finished his thought. "You aren't exactly a stranger in River City, are you?"

"If someone recognized me, they could connect me to Laura." It was possible his past had already hindered his ability to keep Laura safe.

But his pal was quick to reassure him. "Unlikely. River City has grown by leaps and bounds since your days there. Unless there's something you need to tell me?"

He knew what Blake was alluding to. His friends had pulled him from that gambling life after he'd lost everything, including his ranger career, to it. The addiction had overtaken him, tossing him into a deep, dark pit of despair. They'd all had their ways of coping with the aftermath of the ambush. That had been his.

"No. Except for meetings, I never go near there." His Gamblers Anonymous meetings were held at a church on the outskirts of town. It was a small connection to his old life, but it was one he still considered important.

Colton was certain he heard relief in Blake's voice. He knew how bad he'd gotten and Blake, the closest of his ranger brothers, had had a front-row seat for his descent. "For now, keep a low profile. I'll swing by and we'll see if we'll take a look at the area. We might be able to find some bullet fragments or tire tracks that could lead us to the shooter."

"We'll be here. Can I ask one more favor? Laura didn't have time to pack a bag and we left the store before purchasing anything. Do you think Miranda would mind lending her some clothes?" They'd left behind the groceries as well, but he still had a full freezer, so they would be okay food-wise.

"Sure, I'll ask her."

Colton thanked him, then hung up. His friend wouldn't let him down. The bond they shared was something that could never be erased. Because no matter what he did or where he went, his ranger brothers would always have his back.

Blake arrived at the house later that afternoon with Miranda by his side. Colton and Laura met them on the porch. Laura saw Blake had an air of former military about him. Miranda was pretty, blonde and petite, but her jewelry suggested a flamboyant personality.

"Laura, this is Blake Michaels. We were in the Rangers together. And you've already met Miranda."

"It's nice to meet you," Laura said, extending her hand to Blake.

Blake shook her hand, but Miranda wrapped Laura in a hug instead. "Oh, Laura, Blake told me what's happened to you. I'm so sorry. Don't you worry. I brought plenty of clothes and stuff that you're welcome to borrow."

"Thank you. I appreciate your help."

"Don't think anything about it. We're always here for one another, aren't we, Blake?"

"That's right. The Rangers are a band of brothers. We're always there to help."

Blake pulled out a sheet of paper. "I've been doing some checking into Chuck Randall's background. You were right, Colton. He's a dangerous man. He's a suspect in a string of gaming schemes, drug deals and brutal assaults. It's even reported that he has mob connections. He's a man used to getting whatever he wants."

"And now he wants me," Laura stated, fear rippling through her at Blake's list of Randall's corrupt deeds.

"We're not going to let that happen," Colton assured her.

Blake was more direct. "We're going to do everything in our power to keep you safe. But first we need to understand how he knew where you were. I'd like to check out where the shooting happened. If we can find shell casings or tire marks, we may be able to take molds and match the type of tires the shooter had on his vehicle. It may help identify him."

Miranda wrapped her arm around Laura's good shoulder and smiled. "You two go ahead. We're going to try on some clothes and maybe whip up some supper. We'll be fine."

The men gathered their guns. Miranda kissed Blake, making him promise to be safe, before the men walked out the door.

Colton readied the alarm, then turned to Laura. "Lock this door behind us and call my cell phone if you see someone lurking around. We won't be more than a few minutes away."

Laura watched at the window as they mounted ATVs and headed out in the direction of where the shots had come from.

When they were gone, Miranda promised her, "They'll find something. Blake is the best investigator in the state. And Colton...well, he is nothing if not persistent."

Laura noticed the ring on Miranda's finger and how

happy she and Blake seemed. "How long have you and Blake been together?"

"We both grew up together here in Compton and started dating in high school. We broke up for a while when he joined the army, but then we started writing back and forth and rekindled the romance. We were supposed to get married nearly three years ago. Had our wedding all planned out. Then the ambush happened."

"The ambush?"

"Blake and Colton's ranger squad was ambushed. All but six of them died that night in Afghanistan. Those that made it ended up injured and scarred for life. That night changed him. When he was released from the hospital, all he wanted to do was come back home and mourn what he'd lost. Blake's slowly gotten his life back together, but he never rejoined the Rangers. He retired from the army and took a job here with the sheriff's office." She looked at Laura, then blushed. "I don't know why I'm telling you all of this. I hardly know you, but you seem kind. And Colton likes you, so that's good enough for me."

Laura was stunned to learn Colton had been caught up in an ambush. She'd suspected he'd suffered loss in his ranger squad, but she'd never expected this. She glanced at the photo of the rangers. There were at least twenty men in that photo and to know only six were left alive made Laura shudder. Colton had certainly suffered loss and suddenly her anger toward her father seemed petty in comparison.

"Now, let's see if we can find something else for you to wear." Miranda hauled the suitcase she'd brought upstairs, placed it on the bed and unzipped it. She pulled a blouse and slacks out and showed them to Laura. "These will look cute on you. Why don't you go try them on and let me see?"

Although the blouse was flashier than she would normally wear, it looked as if it would fit, and Laura was glad for the change of clothes. Colton's T-shirts were way too big. She went into the bathroom and slipped on the blouse. It felt soft against her skin and she felt like a woman again thanks to the soft pastel color.

Miranda squealed with excitement when Laura emerged wearing the new outfit. "Wait until Colton sees you in this. You'll knock his boots off."

She felt herself blush and wondered if she was that obvious. She couldn't deny she was attracted to the handsome former ranger, no matter how hard she was trying to fight it. "How well do you know Colton?"

"I know him well enough to know he won't let anything else happen to you, Laura."

She nodded. "If Colton hadn't been there that night, I don't know what would have happened to me."

"Why does this man want you?"

"I don't know. He's obsessed with me. I never did or said anything to encourage him. But he's determined to have me." Since they were talking so frankly, Laura decided to ask Miranda a personal question. "Did Colton leave the Rangers because of the ambush?"

"He did."

"I had no idea," Laura said. Her heart broke at the story. How Colton must have struggled with such loss.

And yet he still had it inside him to reach out to help others, to help her. He really was a warrior.

"That one event really messed them all up. Colton spent six months in rehab before locating here and buying this ranch."

Six months in rehab? He must have been severely injured in the ambush if it had taken that long for him to recover. It had to have been such a long, hard road for him, yet he still was willing to help her.

She wanted to believe in him when he said he would keep her safe, but she couldn't remember the last time she'd believed in anyone. Was Colton finally the one she could trust to keep his word?

She found herself smiling, then realized it had been a long time since she'd smiled.

They stopped the ATVs and dismounted.

"Where was Laura standing when she was shot?" Blake asked.

"She was here," Colton stated, moving to the spot.

"And where were you standing?"

He hesitated a moment, then took a small step backward.

A knowing grin spread across Blake's face.

"I was showing her how to shoot. Of course I was going to be behind her."

"Of course." His grin spoke volumes.

Okay, so maybe he wasn't fooling Blake with his attraction to Laura, but Blake knew him so well. Hopefully he wasn't broadcasting it to the rest of the world... or to Laura.

"We were here and the shot came from that way," Colton said, pointing out the angle of the bullet. "It grazed her right shoulder."

Blake followed the angle he'd mentioned, searching the ground for evidence of an intruder as he walked. Colton did the same.

"Found something," Blake called and Colton walked over to see tire tracks. "We're fortunate it hasn't rained or been windy today. They look viable." He took out his camera and handed it to Colton. "Take some photos of these while I get the molding kit ready."

Colton snapped several photos of the tracks along with the area. A few feet away he also found shoe imprints and snapped pictures of them, as well.

"How did you get involved with this girl?" Blake asked him.

His pal had never approved of his line of work, but they didn't have time to debate that now. "I met her father in Gamblers Anonymous. That's how I learned she was in trouble. If I hadn't been there, there's no telling where she might be now. She's in real trouble, Blake. I want to help her."

"You know, Colton, I've never known you to let someone sneak up on you that way. Is it possible something else had grabbed your attention?"

He saw where Blake's suggestion was heading. "She's a client. That's all."

"A beautiful client."

"I can't deny it. She's gorgeous. But I also can't let my feelings interfere with my vow to protect her. I can't let my guard down again. He is not going to get her, not on my watch."

Blake chuckled and Colton realized his denials about his attraction to Laura had not been lost on him.

"So what's your plan beyond protecting her? You can't hide forever."

He grimaced. He didn't actually have a long-term plan. All he'd been focusing on was keeping her safe. "That's where I was hoping you could help."

"Well, the logical first step would be to have Randall arrested for attempted kidnapping, but given his background, that's probably easier said than done. I imagine he has more than one corrupt official in his pocket in River City."

"What about the FBI?" Colton prodded.

"Unless he crossed state lines to abduct her, they wouldn't have jurisdiction." Furrowing his brow, Blake asked pointedly, "Besides, why would someone be shooting at her if Randall wants her alive?"

"What do you mean?"

Blake looked him square in the eye. "Is it possible this shooting had nothing to do with Laura?"

"What do you mean? He shot her."

"He might have been aiming for you and hit her instead. When we left the Rangers, we all looked for something else to do with ourselves. You and Garrett started doing search-and-rescue operations. He told me just last week that he'd infiltrated a Taliban camp to rescue two missionaries who'd been taken captive."

"*And?* What are you getting at?"

There was a long pause. "What you and Garrett do

is dangerous. Is it possible someone is looking for revenge for a job you did?"

Colton rubbed his jaw as he considered Blake's suggestion. "No, it's not impossible." Just unlikely. This was about Laura; he was certain of it. Besides, he'd walked away from that life, from those dangerous assignments, more than six months ago in search of something else. He was too old to keep behaving as though he was invincible. He wanted roots, a home, a wife and family...some stability. Helping Laura was the first intervention he'd done since walking away from that life.

But he had to be absolutely sure. "I'll call Garrett and see if he's heard anything."

Was it possible he'd brought Laura into the middle of a revenge plot? Colton had made enemies and those enemies could have found him. As far-fetched as it seemed, it was still an avenue he had to pursue.

Miranda was telling Laura about the way Blake had proposed to her as Laura tried on another outfit. She enjoyed her new friend's chatter. It helped to occupy her mind and seemed so normal that for a moment she could pretend they were just two friends visiting and that some madman wasn't out to abduct her.

Suddenly Miranda stopped talking and leaned her head toward the door as if listening for something.

"What is it?" Laura asked.

"I thought I heard something downstairs."

Laura tensed at the idea. She hadn't heard the ATVs return, so it couldn't be Colton and Blake.

Miranda opened the bedroom door and stood at

the top of the staircase listening. Laura joined her and jerked when she heard something downstairs.

"It's probably just one of the dogs," the other woman stated, trying to reassure her, but Laura knew those that hadn't followed Colton and Blake had been left outside. But if someone was really inside the house, how had they gotten past the dogs?

Miranda took out her cell phone. "I'm phoning Blake." She tried to call but shook her head when he didn't answer. "It went straight to voice mail." She put away her phone and started down the steps.

"What are you doing?" Laura asked urgently.

"I'm going to see who is down there."

"Then I'm going, too," Laura said, following closely behind as they took the stairs.

They reached the bottom and looked around but saw no one. Laura stepped into the kitchen and spun around when she heard Miranda cry out. A man stepped from the closet and grabbed Miranda. Laura rushed to her, only to have another man appear and grab her, too. Laura screamed and struggled against her attacker and saw Miranda doing the same.

The man who held Miranda lost his patience and hit her, knocking her to the floor. She instantly went quiet.

Laura cried out when her friend didn't get up, praying she was okay.

The other man joined her attacker and grabbed Laura's legs. She kicked and flailed against her attackers, screaming as they carried her outside to a waiting car, and she knew she was in real trouble if they managed to get her into that car and drive away. She had no idea who these men were or what they wanted, but she knew they must belong to Randall.

She might never see Colton again if she couldn't get away and the thought galvanized her. She remembered the weapons closet inside the laundry room. If only she could escape their grasp, maybe she could protect herself. She continued to kick and struggle with all her might, but the men were too overpowering as they pushed through the door.

Suddenly she heard the howls of dogs and the sounds of paws on the porch. Milo and Roxie appeared from around the corner, barking and jumping on her attackers. The men swatted and kicked at the dogs, but that only riled them more.

"Stop right there!" Colton's voice boomed through the air and the man holding her spun around at the sound of his voice.

Laura's heart lurched. He'd returned in time to save her.

"Freeze!"

The man spun again at the sound of Blake's voice.

Both men trained their guns on the assailants. Her attackers raised theirs as well, the one holding her pulling her closer to use as a shield.

"Let her go," Colton warned them. "Drop your weapons."

The one holding Laura suddenly shoved her to the ground and both men took off running toward their car. Blake and Colton ran after them.

A moment later Colton and Blake were back by her side.

"They got away."

"Where's Miranda?" Blake demanded.

"Inside. They knocked her out."

At her words, Blake bolted into the house.

Colton helped her to her feet, then wrapped his arms around her. "Are you okay? Did they hurt you, Laura?"

She burrowed her head on his shoulder, savoring his comforting warmth. "No. I'm okay. How did you know we were in trouble?"

"We didn't," he said gruffly. "We were heading back and saw the car."

"How did they know I was here?" she asked.

"I don't know, but we're going to find out."

Blake was helping Miranda to the couch when they entered the house.

Laura saw that Miranda's lip was bloody and swelling was already apparent on her right cheek. She hurried to the freezer, found a bag of frozen peas and took it to her. "Hold this against your cheek. It'll help with the swelling." She checked Miranda's eyes and found them equal and reactive, indicating no concussion. But once she was certain the young woman wasn't seriously injured, guilt rushed in. "I'm so sorry. This happened to you because of me."

"It's not your fault," Miranda insisted. "I'm thankful the guys returned in time."

"Me, too," Laura said, glancing at Colton. She saw the guilt on his face, as well. He was blaming himself and it truly wasn't his fault. He couldn't have foreseen someone would break in while they were out investigating.

She was just so thankful he and Blake had arrived in time.

* * *

Colton walked over to examine the alarm. It was disarmed. He turned back to the two women. "Did one of you turn this off?" They both shook their heads.

Blake stood and approached him. "What is it?"

"The alarm was deactivated. Whoever did it must have known the code."

"Who else knows it?"

"Only a few people. You, Miranda, Tony Hurst, who helps me out on the ranch. My cleaning lady, Evelyn Greer, who comes by to clean twice a month. Plus the people from the alarm company. I had it upgraded a few months ago." He pressed the keys to reset it, then turned to Laura. "Did you recognize either of those men?"

She shook her head, her eyes glassy, still in a state of shock. "No, I didn't know them."

"I did," Blake stated. "It was the McGowen cousins. They're locals who have been in and out of trouble with the sheriff's office for robbery and house burglary."

"It's quite a jump from robbery to kidnapping."

"True, but the reward money Randall is offering could be driving them. I'm going to swear out warrants for their arrest for assault and attempted kidnapping. They're going to pay for putting hands on my fiancée."

Colton saw the fire in his eyes and understood Blake's anger. He felt the same way about the attack on Laura, but he still didn't understand how anyone knew Laura was here at his ranch. How had they tracked her down so quickly?

He thought about what Blake had said about these attacks being for revenge for a job he'd done, but it seemed less and less likely. Those men had come for Laura. They'd knocked Miranda out to get to her. And although he still hadn't figured out how they'd known his alarm code, he was certain Blake had been wrong about that, as well. But he had been correct when he'd advised Colton not to take anything for granted.

He waited until Blake and Miranda left and Laura had gone upstairs after a thrown-together supper to rest before he picked up his cell phone and dialed the number for Garrett Lewis. He and Garrett had served together in the Rangers and shared a continuing mission for serving those in need. Colton had brought the younger man in and together they'd established a private endeavor to help folks out of sticky situations. They'd made contacts in their years in the Rangers and together they'd built a stellar reputation for themselves in many different countries.

Money had flowed in and the jobs had grown bigger and grander. It had given Colton the means to buy this ranch and settle down when the jobs and the pace had gotten too much for him. He'd backed away from the missions, allowing Garrett to take over more and more. The younger man had more of a taste for the risk and danger, and Colton's interest had begun to wane. He'd retreated to this little ranch and the slow pace it provided him.

Garrett answered quickly. "Colt, what's the word?"

"I need some intel, Garrett. I had a shooter on my property. Have you heard anything about anyone seeking revenge?"

"No, I haven't, but I'll keep my ears open."

"I'd appreciate it," Colton said. "Let me know if you hear anything."

"I will."

"Garrett, where are you?"

"North Dakota," the younger man replied. "A woman's family hired me to find and rescue their daughter from a dangerous cult. The leader is one crazy dude."

Garrett had a thing about cults and always took jobs that allowed him to infiltrate and liberate cult captives.

"Are you working on anything right now?" Garrett asked. "'Cause I've got some leads on jobs. We could use your help."

Colton drummed his fingers on the table. Garrett's offer was tempting, but that life just wasn't enough for him anymore. "I don't think so. Not now. I'm helping someone out of a bad situation." He filled Garrett in on everything that was happening, including the shooting and even the earlier attempted abduction. "Blake says he knows the guys from today, but it seems Laura isn't even safe here."

"She has you, Colton, and I know how determined you can be," his pal reminded him. "You'll figure out how to keep her safe. Besides, you know the Rangers always have your back. If you need me, I'll be there."

"I appreciate that, Garrett."

"But yet you don't sound convinced."

He exhaled wearily, scrubbing a hand over his jaw. "Laura is in this situation because of her father and his gambling problem."

"Romans 8:1."

He knew the verse Garrett was referring to. He'd

clung to it during his dark days. "'There is now no con-
demnation for those who are in Christ Jesus.'"

"You're no longer that guy, Colton. You've been
changed. You have to believe that or no one else will."

Garrett's words were just what he needed to hear
and he was happy he'd called him. It amazed him how
well his brothers knew him. Garrett had sensed he was
doubting himself and been right there to pick him up
and remind him of God's grace and mercy.

Laura appeared from upstairs. She walked into the
kitchen and poured herself a cup of coffee, then took the
seat across from Colton. She looked pale and in pain,
but she tried to smile at him.

"I have to go," he told Garrett. "Call me if you find
out something." He hung up the phone and addressed
Laura. "Feeling better?"

"It's not bad," she told him, but the dark circles
around her eyes spoke volumes. She was not only still
hurting from the gunshot, she was worn-out. How many
sleepless nights had she spent worrying about Randall?
Or her father? She needed a good night's sleep. He was
going to make certain no one else got close enough to
harm her.

Laura picked up the photo of Colton and his ranger
friends from its place on the mantel. They appeared to
be a formidable group. She remembered what Miranda
had told her about the ambush and it broke her heart to
think most of these men hadn't made it home.

She looked at him now, his face scrunched as he
stared at the screen of his laptop.

"What are you looking up?" she asked.

"I'm looking into backgrounds of a few people I know—those who might have had access to the house. Blake will be running down their criminal backgrounds, but I want to see if anything pops up that might be a red flag."

"And what have you found?"

He sighed and shut the laptop. "So far, nothing."

She could feel the frustration rolling off him.

"There has to be a connection between the break-in, the shooting and Randall. But how would anyone know you were here? Have you called anyone?"

Her face reddened. He'd specifically asked her not to phone anyone, but she had. She couldn't let people she cared about wonder if something had happened to her. "My friend Denise. She works with me at the hospital. I asked her to let our nurse manager know I was going to be out for a while and I wanted to let her know I was safe. She knows about my father's gambling debts."

He nodded but didn't appear to be angry at her for placing the call. "Anyone else?"

"Only my landlady. She's a very sweet elderly woman. I told her I was going out of town for a while and asked her to feed my cat while I was away."

"Is it possible she told someone?"

"No. She's aware of the trouble I've had with my father. When people started showing up at my apartment wanting money for his debts, she became very protective of me. I think she went through something similar with her late husband." Mrs. Duncan knew about discretion. Like Laura, she was a very private woman.

"Besides, she wouldn't be able to tell anyone anything because I didn't tell her where I was."

"They might have tapped her phone, although I doubt they would have had time since yesterday. They thought they were going to grab you with no problems and were probably scrambling to figure out what to do after that. But if they did in fact trace the call you made to your landlady, all they would have is an approximate location, since my number is unlisted. My theory is that they might have started out at the main shops..." He shook his head, chagrined. "I should have known better than to have taken you there. I'm sorry, Laura. I let you down."

"No, you didn't, Colton. I'm the one who placed the calls. If someone did track us down, it's because of me."

His cell phone rang and Colton glanced at the screen. "It's Blake." He answered, then gave Laura a grim look before reaching for the TV remote. "What channel?"

He clicked on the television and changed it to a station broadcasting the news. Laura saw a reporter standing in front of an apartment building. Police and ambulances were behind her, their lights flashing. Across the bottom of the screen, a message scrolled: Body of Elderly Woman Found Dead in Her Apartment. Another Woman Missing.

Laura realized the building looked familiar. It was her apartment building.

She focused on the words the reporter was speaking and felt her heart drop.

"Again, one woman, seventy-three-year-old Lily Duncan, was found dead in her apartment today. Foul play is suspected in her death and the police are still investigating. Police are searching tonight for Mrs. Duncan's upstairs neighbor, Laura Jackson, who, according to social media posts, went missing two days ago after completing her shift as a nurse at River City Medical Center. We've recently learned her backpack was found in the employee parking lot along with her abandoned car and police suspect foul play. If you have any information about Laura Jackson's whereabouts, please contact the River City Police Department..."

Tears flooded Laura's eyes. Mrs. Duncan was dead, murdered in her home. Had it been because of her? Had Randall sent men to find out if she knew where Laura was?

Colton switched off the television, then pulled Laura into his arms. She went willingly, needing his strength and comfort. This was no coincidence. Her landlady was dead because of her. Did that also mean every one of her friends was in danger, also?

"My father!" Laura gasped. If they would kill Mrs. Duncan because she might know her whereabouts, what would they do to her father or Denise?

Colton was dialing her father's number before Laura could even explain her sudden realization. He must have come to the same conclusion.

He placed the call on speaker as the phone on the other end of the line rang. Finally, after four grueling rings where Laura imagined him lying dead or injured, he answered his cell. "Hello?"

"Dad!" she cried, never before so thankful to hear his voice.

"Laura." The relief was evident in his tone. "It's

good to hear from you, baby. Are you all right? Is he keeping you safe?"

"I—I'm fine, but we just saw on the news that my landlady is dead. She was murdered, Dad. Wh-where are you? Are you okay?"

"I'm fine. I'm staying with a friend."

"Has Randall tried to contact you?" Colton asked.

"He's called, but I haven't answered. And I've tried to stay out of sight. Don't worry. Even if he finds me, he won't get any information from me. You just focus on protecting my daughter."

She looked up from the phone and saw Colton looking at her, determination steeling his gaze.

"Don't worry. I'll keep her safe," he said.

She instinctively knew he would. He'd already proved the lengths he would go to to shield her from harm, and despite the earlier incidents, she felt protected here with Colton. He wouldn't let her down.

She made her father promise to remain hidden, then disconnected the call.

Her dad was okay for now, but Mrs. Duncan had paid the ultimate price for Randall's obsession. The man had just raised the stakes and Laura feared no one in her life would be safe until Randall was stopped.

FOUR

Laura was quiet over breakfast the next morning. Colton could tell she hadn't slept well. The loss of her neighbor had been a big blow and one that he hadn't been expecting. It didn't make any sense to him. If Randall had killed Laura's landlady to try to find out where Laura was hiding, that meant he didn't know about the ranch. But if he didn't know about the ranch, then who had been shooting at them? And why had the cousins tried to abduct her?

As they stood over the sink rinsing off the breakfast dishes, Colton couldn't stand the silence anymore.

"I know you're sad," he said softly. "I'm sorry about your friend."

Laura shook her head. "She wasn't really a friend. She was a very private person. We chatted occasionally, but that was about it. I hardly knew anything about her. I don't even know if she has a next of kin to contact."

"The police will take care of that."

"And will the police tell them that Mrs. Duncan probably died because of me?"

He dropped the plate in his hand and turned to her. "Stop it, Laura. This isn't your fault. This is all Randall's doing. If you're looking for someone to blame, then blame him."

"What exactly is your plan, Colton? For me to hide out here for the rest of my life and hope Randall gets tired and moves on?"

He heard the sarcasm in her voice and didn't appreciate it. He stepped toward her, his expression hard. "Right now, my only plan is keeping you alive. And, believe me, you're not making it easy."

"I'm tired of being locked up inside this house. I want to go home. I want to return to work. I want my life back." She put her hands over her face as she struggled to keep her composure. "It's not fair. I didn't do anything to deserve this. My father is the one who messed up. Why am I the one paying the consequences?"

He saw her tremble and put his arms around her. Regardless of their relationship, someone she knew had been murdered and the killer was now searching for her.

He stroked her hair, loving the softness of her curls and the way it felt against his hand. She glanced up at him, her green eyes full of fear and confusion, her lashes wet with tears. But it was her lips he focused on and the sweet beckoning way they called to him. He pulled his eyes from her lips and found her eyes focused on him, too, her chin lifted and her lips waiting for a kiss.

He pulled away. He couldn't go down that road with someone he knew he couldn't have. Why torture himself? Besides, she was upset and he wasn't one to take advantage of a lady when she was feeling vulnerable.

He cleared his throat, suddenly at a loss for words. "Laura, I—"

She stared silently up at him. For an instant he thought he saw a flicker of disappointment flash in her eyes. Was it possible she'd ached for their kiss as much as he had?

He heard footsteps on the porch and the door suddenly swung open. He was reaching for his firearm when Mrs. Greer appeared in the doorway. He'd forgotten it was her day to come by to clean. Her eyes widened to find him in the embrace of a woman, but her shocked expression quickly turned to gleeful delight.

"I didn't mean to interrupt," she exclaimed. "Should I come back later when you're not so busy?" Her playful glint meant she was happy to see Colton with a woman. She'd been trying to fix him up with every woman in the county since he'd moved to town.

Colton pulled an arm's distance away from Laura. "Mrs. Greer, this is Laura Jackson. I'm helping her out of a sticky situation she's having."

Mrs. Greer smiled, then closed the door and approached them. "Sorry to hear that, love, but I know Colton will take care of things for you."

He turned to Laura. "Mrs. Greer comes in to clean and do laundry."

"That's right, I do. You wouldn't think one man would have so much laundry to do, but this one does. He works too hard around this place and he's got the dirty laundry to show for it. If you have anything you'd like me to wash for you, Laura, just bring it down."

"No, thank you," she said, smiling politely back at her. "I'm fine for now."

"I should probably go work on that tractor. It keeps breaking down on me."

"You go on, Colton. Laura and I will be fine. Maybe she can keep me company while I work. Won't that be lovely?"

"Certainly," Laura agreed.

Colton walked to the door and grabbed his hat. He looked back at the two women already chatting away. He knew Mrs. Greer was probably already playing matchmaker, talking him up to Laura, but he was now more convinced than ever that he couldn't allow anything to happen between them. And it wasn't just the fact that she would never want anything to do with him if she knew about his past.

Mrs. Greer had managed to sneak up on them in his own house. He hadn't even heard her car approach. He couldn't allow that. If Laura Jackson had that kind of effect on him, he would never be able to keep her safe.

Laura tried to help Mrs. Greer with the breakfast dishes, but the woman shooed her away. "This is my job. I don't mind doing it. I've been taking care of Colton now for a while. He's such a nice person. He hired me after my husband passed away. I'd already retired from my job at the courthouse and then Walter got sick and we had all these medical bills. Colton helped me through it. I don't know what I would have done without him."

"I'm sorry about your husband," Laura stated.

"Thank you. I don't know what the problem you're having is, but Colton will help you."

"I hope so. I honestly don't know if anyone can."

"Do you have family?" Mrs. Greer asked.

Laura nodded. "My father. He's actually why I'm in this mess."

"I've lived a lot of years, Laura, and trust me, we all make mistakes. The ones that hurt us aren't so bad. We go on. But it's the ones that hurt those we care about that follow us for the rest of our lives. I'm sure whatever your father did to you, he regrets it."

Laura hung her head. Her father had tried to apologize, but she hadn't wanted to hear it. She still didn't want to hear it. She wanted to hold on to her anger. It was the only thing that was keeping her from falling apart.

"It doesn't matter that he regrets it," she told Mrs. Greer. "It doesn't make things any better."

She didn't like the look Mrs. Greer gave her. It was as if the older woman felt sorry for her. Why did she need to be pitied for not forgiving her father? He was the one who had messed up, not her.

Milo bounded at her feet as Laura stepped outside. She reached down and scratched the dog behind his ear. She'd taken a liking to this old mutt. In fact, she'd taken a liking to this entire place. Smiling despite herself, she thought about how Colton had described this as a peaceful haven and it really was. It was a slowdown from all she knew, a refreshing change of pace from the way she'd lived her entire life, and it was a good change.

But sitting around doing nothing was driving her

crazy. She was used to hard work and she needed to occupy her mind. There had to be something around here she could do to keep herself busy.

"Let's go, boy," she said and he trotted along behind her as she headed toward the shop, where she figured Colton would be if he was working on the tractor. She walked inside and didn't see him. Strange. He'd said he would be out here, but the shop was empty.

She heard a noise and turned. "Colton?"

Laura started out the door. She jumped at the figure in the doorway, a tall, muscular man wearing work clothes and a baseball cap.

She backed away from him, fear rippling through her. She shouldn't have left the safety of the house. "Who are you?" she demanded. He'd sneaked up on her so silently—or had he already been there waiting for her and watching? "What do you want?"

"I came in for a wrench," he said, moving past her to the workbench of tools. He grabbed a wrench, then held it up for her to see. "I work for Colton. My name is Tony Hurst. You must be the lady he's helping out."

Relief flooded her and Laura felt her face flush at the realization she'd jumped to conclusions. "Tony. Yes, hello. It's nice to meet you. I'm Laura. Laura Jackson."

"Nice to meet you, ma'am."

"Do you know where Colton is? I thought he was going to be out here."

"He's out back, behind the barn. That old tractor started fine but then conked out on us. I was getting this for him. If you're going out there, you can take it to him."

"Sure." She took the wrench from him.

"Tell him I'm heading out to the pasture. I'll catch up with him later."

She walked around to the back of the barn and found Colton squatting, working on the tractor. Mesmerized, she watched the way the muscles in his arms pressed against his tight T-shirt as he lifted a heavy object. He was strong and physically fit. She could imagine him storming in raids. It was an attractive vision. She pushed those thoughts from her head. Yes, he was handsome and powerfully built, and he'd swooped in and rescued her, but she'd been let down too many times by the men in her life. She wouldn't make that mistake again.

He wiped grease from his hands with a rag and turned to see her standing there. "Hey, Laura, what are you doing out here?"

"I have something for you," she said, handing over the wrench. "I met Tony. He said he would see you later."

"Okay, thanks." He set the wrench aside. "Laura, you should stay inside the house. It might not be safe out here, especially alone."

"I need something to do, Colton. I don't enjoy being idle. There must be something I can do to help around here. This is a ranch, after all."

"It's not necessary. You should take it easy, relax. I know you need to sleep."

"I can't relax and I can't sleep. I need to keep busy. It helps to keep my mind off what's happening." She blew out a breath. "Without something to occupy my thoughts, I'm going to drive myself crazy with worry."

He must have seen her frustration because he finally gave in. "I could use some help in the barn, cleaning out the stalls. It'll keep you busy and I'll be close by so I can keep an eye on you."

"I'll do it."

He led her to the barn and showed her the rack of tools that included a broom, a shovel and a pitchfork, then walked her through the steps for cleaning each stall.

"Are you sure about this?" he asked, giving her another opportunity to back out. She could see he wanted her to spend her days lazing around as if she was on a vacation or at a retreat and not in a fight for her life. But that wasn't who she was. She needed to stay busy and mucking out the stalls was just the kind of physical work that could keep her mind off her troubles.

She took the broom from his hand. "I'm sure. This is just what I need."

She got to work, glad to have something to occupy her mind, and realized she was less on edge here with Colton than she had been in weeks. That said something. She felt comfortable here, but she had to be careful. Couldn't get *too* comfortable. She had to look out for herself.

As she was finishing up the last stall, Colton appeared, leaning against the railing and watching her. "Is this what you had in mind?"

Laura wiped sweat from her forehead and laughed, knowing she must look horrible from the sweat and muck, and probably smelled even worse, but she felt good. "I do feel better," she admitted "It feels good to accomplish something."

"Blake phoned. He has some information about Mrs. Duncan's murder. He and Miranda invited us over for supper."

"That sounds great. I like Miranda. It's nice to have another woman to talk to."

"Great. I'm going to shower and change. You should, too." He smirked at her, then winked.

She couldn't help but smile at his wit. Could anyone else basically tell her she smelled bad without putting her down? She watched him stride back to the house and realized he did more than make her feel safe…he also made her feel good about herself. And that was something she hadn't felt from anyone in a long, long time.

Colton enjoyed watching Laura interact with Miranda. The two women seemed to have bonded quickly and he liked spending time with her. He could imagine many more meals with him and Laura and Blake and Miranda. It was like the perfect life he'd always dreamed of but knew would never happen for him. It still wouldn't. He had to remember that. Laura had no idea who he was. When she discovered the truth about his past, any future he could envision for them would be over before it even started. Better not to even hope for it.

After dinner, he joined Blake on the front porch and Blake caught him up on what he'd found.

"So I did some digging into the River City police. The detective in charge of Laura's neighbor's death is named Merle. He's been with the RCPD for two years, but he's a ten-year veteran of the US Navy. I placed a few calls and, from what I can tell, he seems to be on the up-and-up. I'm going to call him and see if I can find out any information about the murder. See if they have anything connecting Randall to it."

"He'll want information on Laura," Colton said in a low, worried tone. "What if he wants her to return to River City to give a statement?"

"I'll do what I can to keep that from happening, but we may have no choice, Colton. And I would rather go to them than have them come to us. We have a better chance of keeping Laura's location a secret if we take her back to make her statement."

A muscle ticked in his jaw. "If this guy Merle is in Randall's pocket, it won't matter one way or the other. Either way, we'll be in trouble."

"I'll do my best to feel him out."

"I trust your best, Blake. I'm just concerned." He stared through the window into the house, where Laura was talking and smiling with Miranda.

"I know you are. It's only been a few days and she's already gotten under your skin, hasn't she?"

"She has in a big way." He saw Blake's grin, but he didn't find it the least bit amusing. "It's a real problem," he grumbled. "This morning, Mrs. Greer was inside the house before I even realized it. What if that had been one of Randall's men?"

"Well, Mrs. Greer did work as a constable for years before she retired. I imagine she got good at sneaking up on people who didn't want to be served with papers.

And you know she drives that little scooter thing that doesn't make much noise."

He felt a sudden urge to wipe that annoying smirk off his friend's face. "I've got to keep my focus on protecting Laura," he bit out. "She's really shaken up over the death of her neighbor. She blames herself, since the men were after her."

"Actually, buddy, we don't know that yet. You're both jumping to conclusions. It might turn out to be a simple break-in that Mrs. Duncan interrupted."

Colton hoped his friend was right. Mrs. Duncan's death was a tragedy, but linking it to Randall and his obsession for Laura would make an already dangerous situation even that much worse. If Randall was willing to kill an elderly woman to get to Laura, there was no telling what else he might do.

One more reason for Colton to keep his wits about him and not let his attraction to Laura distract him.

Colton was quiet on the drive back to the ranch. Laura had noticed the men slip away onto the porch after supper and wondered if their conversation had prompted his terse mood.

When they were back at the ranch, she broached the subject. "I can see something is wrong, so you might as well tell me."

He gave her a slight grin. "Think you can read me that well, do you?"

"You're obviously on edge."

He rubbed his face and sighed before he broke the

news to her. "Blake says the lead investigator into Mrs. Duncan's death may want to question you."

She took her cue from Colton. He looked worried, so she was worried, too. "You don't think I should?"

"I'm hesitant. Randall is a powerful man in River City. There's no telling how many of the police are on his payroll. I could be delivering you right into his clutches." He clenched his jaw and Laura could once again feel how important her safety was to him. "Blake assures me he'll talk to the detective. He doesn't believe he's a dirty cop, but..."

"But what? You don't trust Blake's judgment?"

"Without a doubt I trust his judgment, but anyone can be fooled, Laura. Even the Rangers."

She sensed an underlying reference in his words and knew he was thinking about the ambush. They'd trusted someone who had betrayed them all.

"What if we don't go? What will happen?"

He shrugged. "The police will be spinning their wheels looking for Mrs. Duncan's killer without all the necessary information. Plus, they'll keep looking for you. You're on the police radar now. But if we do go and Randall owns the police..." He leaned against the kitchen island, obviously wrestling with this decision. Finally he turned back to her. "I think you should do it. When it comes down to it, I trust Blake. If he believes the detective can be trusted, we go."

She saw Colton still had his doubts, but he chose to believe in his friend. She wished she could trust as easily has he did. What would it be like to have someone in your life who you believed in so completely?

She stopped, momentarily stunned to realize that she did have someone in her life like that. She had Colton.

She nodded. She would trust his judgment. "I'll go, but I want to do something while we're in River City."

"What's that?"

"I want to go to my apartment."

He was shaking his head before she'd even completed her sentence. "That's not a good idea."

"I want to see Mrs. Duncan's apartment and I want to check on mine. My cat is still there. She's probably frightened. Mrs. Duncan was going to feed her and clean the litter box. I need to check on her."

"It's not a good idea, Laura. Randall's men may be watching your place in case you come back."

"I doubt they're hanging around the scene of a murder they've committed. Besides, you'll be with me and I trust you to protect me if that happens. I need to do this, Colton. Please say you'll come with me."

He gazed at her and she hoped he saw the determination in her face. She needed to see her apartment and check on Misty, and if they had to go to town to meet the detective, then there was no reason not to do so.

He finally gave in and agreed. "I don't think it's a good idea, but I'll go along with you."

Laura stared at the opening of her neighbor's door. Crime scene tape still cordoned it off, but the front door was broken and she could see evidence of a struggle inside. She was so sad about what had happened to Mrs. Duncan. She hadn't done anything wrong…except perhaps stand up to her attackers. Mrs. Duncan was a strong lady and Laura knew she wouldn't have backed down quickly. She'd probably had a few choice words to say to the men who'd broken into her home.

The police might have an idea of what had happened, but all Laura had was a vision of Mrs. Duncan fighting for her life. Had she interrupted Randall's men ransacking Laura's apartment? Or had they targeted her for what she might know? Had they meant to kill her or had things escalated? She shook away those questions. None of them mattered. A woman she cared for was dead. Guilt and anger welled up inside her once again. Her father's choices continued to affect others and Mrs. Duncan had paid the ultimate price.

Colton nudged her, pulling her out of her reverie. "It doesn't do any good to beat yourself up over this. It wasn't your fault."

He could keep saying that all he wanted, but it didn't stop Laura from feeling responsible. Still, she headed up the stairs to her apartment. She'd lost her keys in the hospital parking lot, so she'd stopped by the apartment office and gotten a spare set.

"I don't like this," Colton told her again. "We shouldn't be here. Randall's men might be watching this place."

She turned the key in her lock. "I image they're staying far away from here. They're wanted for questioning in a murder, remember? Besides, you're here to protect me."

She opened the door and stepped into her apartment. She'd expected it to be trashed, but she was shocked by the manner of things. Randall's men had torn it up. Every drawer in her kitchen had been pulled out and dumped on the floor, causing her utensils to scatter across the floor. Her furniture had been overturned, her plants unpotted and even her television busted. She felt violated at the condition of her home and was glad Colton was there with her. This intrusion tarnished the safety of her little home. She'd always considered this place her sanctuary, but now it was anything but. Randall had managed to run her right out of her home. She doubted she could ever feel safe enough to return here now after what had happened to Mrs. Duncan.

"They must have been looking for a clue to where you might run to."

Laura picked clothes off the floor as she moved through the apartment heading toward the bedroom, which had been equally trashed. She picked up a suitcase that used to be stored inside her closet, hoisted it onto the bed and started stuffing clothes into it. Afterward, she also grabbed several personal items from the bathroom, a photograph book with her mother's pictures, a crocheted blanket her grandmother had given her and several other sentimental pieces.

"Where's Misty?" she asked, glancing around the apartment. She hadn't seen her since they'd walked inside.

"Misty?"

"My cat. She must be hiding." She noticed the door. Misty wasn't fond of strangers and there was no telling how she might have reacted when men she didn't know barged into her home. "I hope she didn't run out when these men did this."

Colton started looking around as Laura called Misty's

name. Terrible thoughts raced through her mind about what could have happened to her cat. She checked in all of her usual hiding places but couldn't find her. If they'd hurt her… She shuddered to think of it.

Colton pulled out his cell phone. "I'll phone Blake and have him find out if any of the police officers saw a cat wandering around the crime scene."

Laura nodded, hoping wherever Misty had wandered, someone was taking care of her. She finished gathering her things while Colton placed the call.

"Well?" she asked when he hung up.

"Sorry…nothing about a cat. But he did say they're ready for us."

She finished gathering her things and Colton carried them downstairs to the truck. Knowing she'd done all she could here, she turned her attention to the upcoming meeting. She still wasn't sure about meeting this detective. She'd heard Randall had the police in his pocket. "Did Blake say anything about this detective?"

"He still thinks he's okay." He rubbed her arms reassuringly and she was glad he was with her. "Are you ready for this?"

Laura took a deep breath, then let it out. She was determined to push through this and trusted Colton's judgment about this man. All they could do was step out in faith and deal with the fallout. "I am. If I can do anything to help bring Randall down for Mrs. Duncan's death, I want to do it."

He nodded and opened the truck's passenger door for her. She slipped inside, and as he closed it, she hoped this unknown detective wasn't luring them into a trap.

* * *

Laura shuddered as Detective Merle gave her a cold, hard stare. He looked intimidating and distrustful as he listened to her recount how her father owed Chuck Randall and how Randall had demanded she marry him to repay his debt. He didn't flinch when she told him about his obsession with her and the attempted abduction in the hospital parking lot. She glanced at Colton standing against the wall with Blake, both men looking as if they were silently summing up the detective.

"What happened to Mrs. Duncan?" Laura asked Detective Merle once she was done telling her tale.

He opened a file and skimmed through it. "According to the autopsy, her throat was slashed. We believe she saw her attackers leaving your apartment and confronted them. The report suggests she was bound for quite a while before she died."

Laura put her elbows on the table and placed her hands over her face as the detective explained the horrible encounter Mrs. Duncan suffered. "It's not fair," she wept. "She didn't know where I was. She had no involvement in any of this."

"Do you have any evidence that could place Randall or any of his men in her apartment?" Colton asked him.

"Not yet," the detective replied. "We're still running fingerprints. Whoever committed this crime was a professional. Can you think of any reason someone might want to hurt your landlady?"

Laura nodded, but her voice was quivering as she answered. "To hurt me."

Colton came over and put a comforting hand on her

shoulder. "They could have also been trying to determine if she knew where you were hiding," he stated.

Detective Merle nodded. "That would seem to fit the evidence better."

"Th-they tortured her," Laura said brokenly. "Th-they tortured her to get to me."

"Laura, none of this is your fault," Colton told her.

"Yes, it is. If I hadn't run… If I hadn't refused Randall…"

"Stop talking that way," Colton demanded. "You didn't do anything."

"I was selfish. I was only thinking of myself, just like my father. I can fix this. I have friends, Colton. Their lives might be in danger, too, and I won't let that happen."

She was determined to make this right. She wouldn't see anyone else suffer the way Mrs. Duncan had because of her. Her father had placed her in this mess, but it didn't mean she had to continue to be a victim. She could stand up and take responsibility. She could give in to Randall's advances and maybe stop his tirade.

"Stop trying to hog all the blame, Laura," Colton chided. "There's plenty to go around. First and foremost, this is Randall's responsibility as well as the men that follow his orders. They're the ones culpable, if you're looking to assign blame."

"I don't want anyone else harmed because of me, Colton. Can't you understand that I wouldn't be able to live with myself if that happened? It doesn't matter what happens to me. I don't have any more family besides my dad. No one will care what happens to me."

He grabbed her arms, his fingers digging into her skin. "I care, Laura. I care about you."

She saw the pain on his face, but at least she wasn't putting his life in jeopardy any longer. "I'll pay you whatever I can. You can have my things and sell them for whatever you can get as payment."

"Stop it, Laura," he growled. "I don't care about the money. I care about you. I won't let anything happen to you and I won't let you give up."

"How are you going to keep me safe, Colton? How are you going to keep my friends and family safe? Randall is everywhere. He owns everyone and everything for miles."

"He doesn't own me."

"Or me," Blake stated.

Even Detective Merle stood. "He doesn't own me, either, Laura. You can trust me. I promise I will do whatever I can to connect Randall to this murder. The sooner he's in prison, the sooner you'll be safe." He turned to Colton. "Take her home. Watch over her. I'll do my best to find evidence linking Randall to this murder. I'll be in touch when I know something."

FIVE

Colton loaded the truck and drove to the north pasture. He needed to repair a fence out there and Laura had asked to come and help however she could. He obliged her request, glad to keep her close by even while he had to work. After the incident when the McGowen cousins had broken into the house, he didn't like leaving her alone even for a little while.

Somehow, and he hadn't figure out how yet, rocks seemed to grow up out of the ground, which made mowing and keeping grass in the pastures difficult. If Laura really wanted to be helpful, he supposed he could have her clear away the stones while he tended to the fence.

"You really don't have to do this," Colton told her. "It's tedious work."

"But it's necessary, right?"

"Yes. We had high winds a couple of weeks ago, so the field will be littered with limbs and branches. We can't run the tractor through it until all that's picked up, which means we can't cultivate the field for pasturing."

She pulled on a pair of gloves. "Then let's get to it."

He admired her tenacity and work ethic. She understood the need for hard work.

Colton worked as fast as he could to mend the fence while keeping an eye and an ear alert for movement around them. The last time they'd been out in the open this way, someone had shot at them, and he wanted to finish and get back inside as soon as possible. When he was done, he pulled two bottles of water from the cooler and walked over to her. As she tossed a heavy rock into the already loaded cart, he handed her a bottle.

"Let's take a break."

"But I'm not done."

"Ranch work is never done, darlin', but we have to take care of ourselves, too, to keep working. Besides, I think we've been out in the open too long."

She pulled off her gloves, took the bottle of water and drank from it, then followed him to the truck and got inside.

"There's no question that it's lovely here," she said softly. "But you must have traveled all over the world with the Rangers. Could have settled anywhere really. Why here?"

He waved his hand over the horizon outside the glass. "Because of this. Look how incredible this place is. I spent years of my life in places torn up by decades, sometimes even centuries, of war. Then I saw this place and all of God's majestic beauty. It's peaceful here and that's what I was looking for. That's what I needed. That's what I still need…"

His voice trailed off, and he found himself lost in thought for several long moments. But he snapped out of his reverie when she reached out and gently squeezed his shoulder, prompting him to continue.

"Sometimes my brain gets so scrambled with all I've seen and all I've done. When I left the Rangers, I couldn't shut it off, all the battles and the fighting. Then Blake invited me here to his hometown and there was something about these hills and these landscapes. It drew me in. It reminded me that there is more to life than the struggle and war. So I decided this was where I wanted to settle down, raise a family, spend my life."

She smiled. "That's actually beautiful. I understand how you feel with life so chaotic. I feel like I'm always running, always putting out fires…even before all this with Randall began. How long were you a ranger?"

"Ten years. I enlisted in the army right out of high school. It's all I had ever known and I honestly never thought I would see a day when I wouldn't be a ranger."

"Miranda told me about the ambush," she said instead, causing him to tense and wonder what else Miranda had told Laura.

"She did?"

"She said you lost men. Most of your squad. I saw the picture of them. I can't imagine how terrible that loss was for you."

"It was awful." His voice cracked as he spoke and it amazed him that that event still had such a pull over him.

"We don't have to talk about it if you don't want to," she said quietly, obviously hearing the raw emotion in his voice.

He quickly reassured her. "It's okay, Laura. It feels

good to talk about it with someone." And it did. He'd held back that wall of pain for too long.

"What happened?"

He thought back to that terrible night on the mountain. He still saw the faces of every one of his brothers who didn't make it off that mountain. "Our interpreter turned out to be a spy for the other side. He led us right into a trap. We had twenty men go into camp that night. Only six of us made it out alive."

He wanted to open up to her, to share how bad he'd gotten, how he'd turned to gambling to drown out any feeling and deal with his grief, but he didn't. He knew it would frighten her away from him and compromise his ability to keep her safe. But he wanted—longed—to share this major event in his life with her. "I went to a really dark place afterward. The army shrinks called it survivor's guilt and I guess they were right, but it didn't stop my free fall into darkness."

"How did you get out of that?" Laura asked curiously. "You're obviously not still in that dark place."

"It was all God's doing. He pulled me up, healed me and delivered me from it.

"I was never what you would call a religious man. I believed in God and had walked the aisle as a teenager. But somehow that had all faded away over the years. I could talk the talk with the best of my ranger friends who were devout believers, but I know now it was all talk." He sighed. "When it came right down to it, I didn't trust God. How can you trust someone who lets you down like that? Who allows men with families to die while allowing me to live? Not one of us came home unscathed. We were all changed that night."

"You questioned how you could trust a God that let you down, but now it seems like you believe in Him again. I see you reading your Bible. What changed?"

"It wasn't something that happened quickly. At first, I was so angry at the situation and at God. I tried to pretend I wasn't, but I stopped reading my Bible. I even left my Bible in a camp in Afghanistan. I abandoned it there, I guess, because I felt abandoned myself there. But I couldn't escape the giant hole of grief and pain and emptiness that lived inside me." He took a long, deep breath, still amazed by how far he'd fallen. "I spent a long time trying to fill it with other things. I even started doing these rescue missions with Garrett because of the thrill of danger it gave me. It helped to fill it, but only for a short while."

"Why? What happened?"

"I hit rock bottom. I thought I had lost everything that ever mattered to me. Then Blake and the other rangers pulled me up. They probably saved my life. I was on a path of self-destruction, taking anyone in my path with me."

"I envy you," Laura said. "You have someone in your life that you can truly count on."

"I have more than one," Colton told her. "I have five former ranger brothers that I could call on at any time and they would be there to help me in a heartbeat. And I would be there for them. I trust them all completely."

He would be there for her, too, he wanted to tell her. She could trust in him 100 percent. But he didn't speak the words. Instead he watched as the afternoon sunlight glistened off her auburn hair. She was so beautiful and he wished he could offer her all this place and all this beauty. But she deserved so much more than a washed-up cowboy like him could ever give her.

Laura's heart broke upon hearing such a tragic story. Colton had fought to keep his composure the whole time, and although she realized he always tried to appear stoic and strong, he still held so much of his pain inside. He didn't allow it to spill out, but she knew one day it would. It had to. And if he didn't allow it to, that pain would manifest itself in destructive ways.

She understood that path of destruction he'd fallen into. It reminded her all too well of a similar road her father had descended. She was glad Colton had made it through, and it sparked a tiny flicker of hope in her. If he could turn his life around, was it possible that her father could change, too?

However, Colton still had not explained how he'd overcome one hurdle. "But how did you get past being angry at God? He allowed this terrible thing to happen to you. How could you ever forgive Him?"

Colton turned to look at her and she thought he could probably see right through her question. How could *she* ever forgive God for allowing all this to happen to her?

"It wasn't easy, but I realized I was being held captive by my anger and bitterness. I was barreling down that path of self-destruction on the sled of anger and despair." He swallowed, his Adam's apple bobbing up and down. "The Bible speaks of God's goodness and love for His children over and over. I chose to believe in it. That's it. It was a conscious choice on my part. And I'm still fighting it, but every time a negative or destructive thought enters my mind, I remind myself that I believe in God's goodness."

"I don't know," she said. "I still don't understand how God could have allowed this to happen to me."

"God didn't put you in this situation, Laura. There is evil in this world. No one knows that better than I do. I've seen it. I've watched it in action. And bad things happen because of that evil. That's not the fault of God, but of man and his evil nature. What I've learned is that God is there like a father to pick us up, dust off the dirt and pull us into His arms to comfort us."

She shook her head, still not convinced. "I still don't know. I'm in this situation because of someone else's actions."

"I know it's difficult, but not being able to forgive is a chain that keeps you bound."

"He doesn't deserve my forgiveness."

"No one ever does. But that didn't stop Jesus from dying for us and offering us forgiveness before God."

"That's easy for you to say."

"No, it's not," he said in a low, guttural tone. "It's never easy. It's a constant struggle. Every day I wake up and have to remind myself that I've chosen to forgive. It's not easy, Laura, but it is worth it."

She remained quiet, thinking about all he'd said as they drove back to the shop to unload. Colton lifted the roll of fence wire to his shoulder and carried it inside. She picked up the bags of tools and followed him. Tony was inside the shop working on the tractor when they entered. Colton waved to him and Tony waved back.

"I got that fence in the north pasture repaired," Colton told him. "Hopefully it'll stay intact for a while. And Laura was a big help picking up rocks."

Tony nodded appreciatively. "That'll make our job easier when it's time to ready that pasture."

"We're going to unload this stuff, then go to the house and fix some supper. Care to join us?"

Tony shook his head. "I appreciate that, but I'm heading home, too. See you both tomorrow."

"'Bye, Tony," Laura called. She watched him walk out, then followed Colton to a doorway near where Tony had been working on the tractor. She stepped over the threshold and saw that it was a small storage room where he kept tools and small equipment.

"Just set those on the workbench," Colton instructed her. "I'll put them away."

Colton hauled the roll of fencing from his shoulder into a bin in a corner. He pulled off his work gloves, then turned to her and smiled. "How about we put those away, then call it a night?"

She started to agree, but before she could, the storage room door slammed shut, trapping them inside.

Colton looked at the door in shock, then turned to Laura. "Must have been the wind," he told her. He walked to it and tried the knob, but it didn't turn. He tried again. "It's locked."

"From the outside?"

"We lock it because we keep tools in here. There was

a rash of thefts several months ago." He heard the tractor fire up and knew someone was there. Tony must have returned. He pounded on the door and called for Tony, but there was no response from the outside.

"Can you call someone to let us out?"

He patted his pockets. "I must have left my phone in the truck."

She rubbed at her eyes that were suddenly burning and stinging and her throat was dry.

Colton pulled on the doorknob again, then pounded on the door. He suddenly realized fumes were coming in under the door. The tractor was parked beside the storage room and the fumes were venting right inside.

He yanked off his top shirt, tearing it in two pieces and placing one over his face. He handed Laura the other piece. "Cover your mouth and nose."

Panic began to rise in her at the worry she saw in him.

"We have to get out of here."

"What's happening?" she asked.

"The tractor exhaust is venting in under the door. It can cause burns to your eyes, skin and lungs. It can restrict our breathing and then…" He didn't say the rest, but she could fill in the blanks. If they didn't find a way out, they'd lose consciousness and suffocate. "Can't you shoot the door open?"

"That wouldn't be a good idea. I don't want to spark any of the fumes."

"Then what do we do?" she asked as fear lit through her voice. "How do we get out of here?"

"We've got to get this door open."

His eyes blurred and his grip faltered. The fumes were already affecting him. Colton glanced at Laura and saw her grab for the cabinet. "Are you okay?" he asked.

She nodded. "I'm just a little dizzy."

"It's from the fumes. We have to get out of here before we both pass out." He put his full weight into the door and rammed it with his shoulder once, then again. It didn't budge. "I need something to take that knob off." He fumbled through the tool bench, but his mind was already getting woozy. He was having difficulty thinking and he could see Laura was already growing weak and sleepy. He couldn't let that happen. He had to get her out of there and quick.

He grabbed a crowbar, then stumbled toward the door. He pried it beneath the doorknob. This was going to be a race to see if they could get out before the fumes overtook them or else they were both dead.

He jammed the tool, then kicked at the door with his foot. He pounded again and again. Finally the knob gave and the door swung open. Colton grabbed Laura, who was already close to passing out, scooped her up into his arms and carried her out through the shop door. He waited until he was a few feet away before he breathed in the fresh, clean air of the day. Laura's lips were already turning blue and she was lethargic. She needed oxygen and she needed it now.

He brought her to the truck and got inside, laying her gently on the seat while he jumped in behind the wheel. He had to get her to the hospital. He roared away toward the highway, then grabbed his cell phone from the holder and dialed 9-1-1, promising to meet the ambulance halfway between his ranch and the hospital.

"Hold on, Laura," he pleaded, then gripped the steering wheel and said a silent prayer for her safety. He couldn't lose her now.

He saw the lights of the ambulance before he heard the sirens. He slammed the truck to a stop along the side of the road and scooped up Laura again as the ambulance stopped. One paramedic opened the back doors and snatched the oxygen tank while the other grabbed the gurney.

Colton laid Laura on the gurney. The paramedic checked her oxygen level, then pulled the oxygen mask over her face and turned it on.

"The dispatcher told us what happened. How long was she exposed to the fumes?" he asked Colton.

"I'm not sure. Ten minutes maybe. We tried to cover our noses and mouths, but we also had to get out."

"You were exposed, as well?"

He nodded and the paramedic approached him. "I should check you out, too."

"No, help her."

"We are. She's being given oxygen. Now we need to examine you."

Laura stretched out her hand and clutched Colton's arm. He looked down at her. "Let them check you," she whispered in a hoarse voice.

He obliged and allowed the paramedic to place an oxygen monitor on his finger, then strap a mask over his face as he sat in the back of the ambulance.

He watched Laura on the stretcher and noted the

color seemed to be returning to her face. He imagined his heart was racing so fast that he wouldn't be surprised if the paramedic insisted he go to the hospital to get it checked out. It was finally starting to beat normally. They'd come so close this time. Too close.

And now his mind was thinking back on the incident and wondering how it had happened and why. Had someone been waiting until they passed out to grab Laura? Or had this been an actual attempt to kill them both? He didn't for one moment believe it was an accident. That door hadn't locked on its own and the tractor hadn't been running when Tony had left the shop.

He didn't want to believe Tony was involved, but he couldn't rule it out. Bitterness pulsed through him at the thought that a friend might have betrayed him. It took him back to the ambush in Afghanistan, to the initial discovery of finding out their translator had betrayed them all.

Colton pushed away the offer to ride to the hospital in the ambulance. He pulled off the oxygen mask, his head already clearer from the oxygen, and decided he would drive to the hospital in his truck.

He followed the ambulance, phoning Blake as he drove and asking him to go by the ranch to look for any clues about what had happened. After asking if they were okay, Blake assured Colton he would take care of it, then meet up with them later.

Colton disconnected and tried to push aside the headache that wouldn't go away. He was more determined than ever to find out who was behind this attack. And he prayed his friend wasn't involved.

* * *

Laura was starting to feel better. The oxygen was helping and she could see from the monitor that her levels were getting back to normal. But she was worried about Colton and she was scared. Trapped in that storage room, she'd faced the idea that those might have been her last moments.

She realized now how precious life was and didn't want to waste it. Forgiving her father for the mess he'd made of her life wouldn't be easy. But Colton was right that holding on to her bitterness wasn't serving a purpose. Her life wasn't better because of it. In fact, it was worse. She was tired of being so angry and longed to set it aside to live again. But how did she even do that?

Colton had said it was a choice he'd made. Could it really be that simple? Could she really choose to forgive her father? But did forgiving her father mean that she had to trust him again? She didn't think she could ever allow him to be a part of her life again. She had to protect herself.

She thought of Colton and realized she had someone in her life she could finally believe in and he trusted God. If he could, then maybe she could, too. She closed her eyes and lifted an uncertain prayer toward Heaven.

God, show me how to forgive my father. Help my heart heal.

Colton saw the hospital doors open and Blake and Miranda rushed through. He was glad they were here. He'd been sitting and thinking for hours about the situation and he needed to bounce his thoughts off Blake.

"Where is she?" Miranda asked, concerned.

He motioned toward the door to the observation room and Miranda turned and went inside. He was glad for that, too. Laura and Miranda had hit it off and it was obvious Miranda cared for her.

"Hey, buddy, you okay?" Blake asked him.

He probably looked as bad as he felt, but Colton wasn't about to share that information. "I'm fine," he insisted, sitting.

"How long are you going to sit out here like this?"

"As long as they're keeping Laura here. They're talking about keeping her overnight for observation, but she's insisting she's fine and wants to leave." He looked at his friend. "Did you go by the ranch?"

Blake nodded, then sat beside him. "I did. The storage room lock was busted and the door was standing open. The tractor wasn't running any longer, but the shop stank of fumes. It probably ran out of gas. I opened the roll door to air it out."

Colton straightened suddenly. "The roll door was closed?"

"Yes."

"It was up when we carried the supplies into the shop."

"Are you sure?" Blake asked. "Maybe this was just an accident."

"No," Colton insisted. "This was intentional. That door didn't just happen to lock. The shop doors didn't just happen to close and the tractor didn't just happen to turn on, venting exhaust fumes inside the room. This was no accident, Blake."

"But I thought Randall wanted Laura alive. Why would anyone try to kill her that way?"

"I don't know," he retorted. "Maybe they were waiting for us to lose consciousness, then they would come inside, carry her out and hand her over to Randall."

Blake rubbed his chin, unconvinced. "It seems far-fetched. You could have both died in there."

Colton stood. "Tony was there. He was working on the tractor when we arrived. He said he was heading home, but he could have circled back and locked us in, then started the tractor."

"You think *Tony* might be involved in this?"

Colton sighed. "I think anyone could be involved at this point, so I can't rule out anybody. I don't want to believe it, but Tony has only been with me for a few months and I don't know what's happening in his personal life. I need to talk to him."

"I'll talk to him," Blake insisted, but Colton shook his head.

"No, I want to talk to him. I want to look him in the eye and see for myself if he's being honest." And he would know, Colton thought. He would know if Tony had tried to kill him.

But Blake was having no part of it. "I'm still the law in this town, Colton. A crime has been committed and it's up to me to investigate it." Colton started to protest again, but Blake gave him a sharp reminder. "This is *my* job, Colton. Let me do it. Your job, don't forget, is to watch after Laura and keep her safe. That's an important task and she needs your full attention now."

He reluctantly agreed. Blake was right. As much as he wanted to, he couldn't confront Tony. He had to stay with Laura to make sure no one got close enough to hurt her again.

* * *

The doctor released Laura that same night and she spent the next morning stretched out on the couch with Milo either curled up beside her or asleep on the floor in front of her. She could see Colton needed rest, too, but wasn't taking it. That worried her greatly. She hadn't been the only one inhaling toxic fumes.

They heard a car approaching. Colton grabbed his gun and moved to the window, peeking out. He relaxed when he saw it was only Blake's police cruiser. "It's Blake. He went to talk to Tony last night and question him about locking us in the storage room." He opened the door and let Blake inside.

"Well?" Colton demanded.

Laura sat up on the couch when Blake entered the house.

"Did you talk to him? What did he have to say?"

Blake looked at Laura, then back at Colton. "He was shocked when I told him what happened to you two. He seemed genuinely surprised. I also ran a background check on him and it came back clean. No trouble with the law. Not even a parking ticket. I don't believe he was involved."

Colton raked a hand over his face. She could see he was relieved Tony wasn't involved, but she knew that left them back at square one.

"I have to say, he wasn't too happy when I told him you thought he was involved."

Colton nodded, seemingly unsurprised. No one liked being suspected. "I'll smooth things over with him when he comes to work."

"Did you really believe Tony was involved?" she asked him after Blake left.

"I don't know," he admitted. "I hope not, but I can't be sure. I wish I'd been the one to go question him and I still intend to when I see him. Randall has proved that he and his money can buy off anyone. Tony was there, and for all I know, he could have a mound of debt that needs to be paid."

"If that's the criteria we're using to suspect people, then Mrs. Greer has to be on your list, too. She said she has medical bills from her husband's illness." She was only teasing, trying to lighten the mood, but he took her statement seriously.

He nodded and sat beside her on the couch. "And she knows the alarm codes. She could have turned it off for the McGowen cousins to break in here."

She shuddered. She hadn't thought of that. "They still haven't been found?"

"No. Blake and his men are looking, but they have hit a dead end so far."

"So it could have even been them that locked us in the storage room."

He sighed and leaned back on the couch, weariness touching his face. "It could have been. Truthfully, it could have been anyone. We should do some more target practice when you feel up to it."

Although a gun hadn't helped them escape the storage room, she still thought it was a good idea. "I'm a long ways away from being able to hit a target anytime I want, Colton."

"I hope you never have to use it, but I prefer being prepared to being surprised."

She stared at him, amazed by the warmth in his eyes and the kindness on his face. He reached out to brush a strand of hair from her face and the air seemed to thicken around them. She felt the rise of his heartbeat and the skin under his hand tingled as he tenderly stroked her cheek.

"You are so beautiful," he whispered.

She closed her eyes, readying herself for his kiss. She didn't even stop to wonder if she should allow him to kiss her. She only knew that she would.

It didn't happen. His phone rang, interrupting their moment.

He glanced at the screen. "It's your father," he said. He quickly answered. "Bill, what's going on?"

She saw his expression change to one of concern and confusion. "Bill? Can you hear me? Bill?"

Laura pulled the phone down so she could hear, too. All she heard were low, painful moans. Her stomach tightened. Something was very wrong.

"Dad? What's happened? Are you okay?"

"Where are you, Bill?" Colton asked.

He still didn't respond.

Panic rose inside her.

Suddenly the phone clicked off. Colton looked at her and shook his head and she knew he was thinking the same thing she was—her father was in trouble.

Laura couldn't sit still and Colton couldn't blame her. That call from her father had been ominous. He had no doubt that something had happened, but they also had no way of knowing where Bill was or how to reach him. Normally, Colton would have phoned an ambulance, but Bill had told them he was staying with a friend, so they didn't even know where to send an ambulance. Colton had still called Detective Merle and asked him to send an officer to Bill's apartment to see if he was there. That had been more than two hours ago and Laura hadn't sat still since.

"Do you want something to drink?" He took the iced tea from the refrigerator and offered her a glass.

She shook her head. "No, thank you."

He set down the pitcher and walked over to her, stopping her pacing. He looked at her and rubbed her arms reassuringly. "Laura, you have to stop worrying. I'm sure he's going to be okay."

"Why hasn't Detective Merle called back? It's bad. I know it's bad. We should have insisted Dad come here."

"It wasn't our decision, Laura. I did offer, but he's a grown man and he makes his own choices. We couldn't force him to come."

She folded her arms and he saw anger settle on her face. "One more stupid decision. When does it stop, Colton? When do I get to stop paying for his mistakes? I'm a nervous wreck. It's not fair that he can still do this to me."

He gathered her close and gently stroked her hair when she rested her head on his shoulder. She was worried because she loved her dad, but she was right. It wasn't fair that she had to suffer because of her father. He'd heard people suggest that distancing was the key to surviving, but he knew Laura was too kindhearted to cut her father out of her life. Even when he'd been at his worst, she wasn't the kind of person to run away from a fight.

She jerked away from him when his phone rang. He picked it up from the counter and looked at the caller ID. "It's Merle." He pushed the button and placed it on speaker. "Detective, thanks for calling me back. I have Laura here with me and you're on speaker. Did you find anything?"

"I sent a uniformed officer to your father's apartment, Laura, but he wasn't there and there wasn't any sign of him. However, I also checked with the local hospitals and a man matching your dad's description was brought into the ER two hours ago." There was a long pause. "He was severely beaten and found lying in an alleyway. He was transferred to the ICU. The victim had no identification on him, so I sent an officer to the hospital to confirm his identity through fingerprinting. Your father's prints were on file from a previous DUI arrest. I am so sorry to tell you this…but it's your father, Laura."

Her chin quivered and Colton knew she was fighting to keep herself composed. Colton put his arm around her and pulled her close again. She felt small and fragile in his arms. He spoke into the phone, but he was looking and speaking to Laura as he answered Merle.

"We're on our way."

Laura was quiet on the drive to River City. Colton didn't like taking her out in the open this way, but he knew she needed to be with her father. Being angry at him for the mess he'd gotten her into didn't negate her feelings toward him. She was determined to go, so he was determined to protect her while she did.

He parked and walked with her into the hospital. He started for the information desk, but she kept going straight for the elevator. "ICU is on the fifth floor."

He'd forgotten for a moment that this was her hospital. She worked here and knew the layout. They stepped into the elevator and he punched the button for the fifth floor. But when the doors opened, Laura didn't move to step out.

After several moments Colton took her arm. "Are you okay?"

"I don't know if I can do this," she whispered brokenly. "I don't know if I can stand to see him like this."

"You can do this, Laura. I'll be right here with you." He squeezed her hand and watched as she fortified herself for what was to come. She took a deep breath, then nodded and stepped off the elevator.

The waiting room was crowded and Colton was surprised when someone spoke Laura's name, then several people spilled out to engulf her in hugs and kind words. She'd claimed to be alone except for her father, but he could see from this outpouring that wasn't true. She had many people who cared for her, including a dark-haired woman dressed in scrubs who rushed to her and pulled her into a warm embrace.

"When I heard it was your father that was brought into the ER, I knew I had to stay with him. I tried to call, but I guess you were already on your way here.

I hope you don't mind, but I called your church to let them know."

"Denise, how is he?" Laura asked.

"He's in a coma and the doctors are worried about his breathing."

"I want to see him," she said.

Denise nodded. "I'll take you back." She put her arm around Laura's shoulders and led her away.

Colton started to follow, but the nurse stopped him. "Only two can visit at a time. You'll have to wait out here."

"I'll be fine," Laura assured him, then disappeared behind the double doors leading into the ICU. He wasn't happy to be separated from her, but he supposed she was safe enough inside the intensive care unit.

Colton found himself surrounded by folks he didn't know. Church friends of Laura's tried to introduce themselves. He liked most of them mainly because they'd come to show their support for her. "We've missed seeing her in Sunday school," one woman told him. "Laura has drifted away from us since this mess with her father started."

"You know about her problems with her father?" he asked.

"Well, she's never talked to me about it, but everyone knows about her father's gambling. She's struggled for a while trying to help him. Laura is a nurturer like her mother was."

"You knew her mother?"

"Yes, we were friends. I knew her mother before she died. She was a beautiful woman and Laura reminds me so much of her, only much more jaded. I suppose its natural after all she's been through." The woman hesitated briefly, then went on. "Laura and my son, Lance, dated for a while and I hoped something would happen between them, but I suppose it wasn't meant to be. Sadly, my Lance likes the gaming tables like so many people these days. Laura couldn't see herself getting involved with someone who reminded her so much of her father."

Her words were a harsh reminder for Colton that Laura could never fall for a guy like him.

Before he left her, the woman pulled on his arm. "Please tell Laura I'm praying for her."

"I will. And thank you."

He knew the power of prayer. He also knew Laura needed as many prayers as she could get.

It had to mean a lot to her that so many people had arrived to support her. He knew from experience how important it was to have people who cared. When he was in trouble—drinking and gambling—heading for rock bottom, his ranger brothers had been there to help him up.

Laura might feel alone, but she wasn't.

Denise walked her to the last room in the unit but stopped in front of a closed curtain. She pulled back the curtain and Laura gasped when she saw the figure in the bed. She hardly recognized her father. His face was swollen and discolored from the beating and his head was wrapped in a bandage. The rest of his body seemed to be knitted together with bandages and stitches and

hooked to machines. As a nurse, she was used to seeing the monitors and lifesaving apparatus, but this was
her father and she wasn't used to seeing him this way.
Seeing him unmoving in the bed caused a flash of fear
and grief she hadn't expected.

Stop it, she chided herself. *Stop acting like a little
child afraid of losing her daddy.*

She pushed back the emotion welling inside her and
forced herself to examine him clinically. She glanced
at the machine that monitored his vitals and saw that
his blood pressure was low but his heart rate steady.
Her father appeared to be stabilized, but she knew he
wasn't out of the woods yet. He was still in danger of
succumbing to his injuries and would remain in ICU
until he regained consciousness and was stable enough
for the breathing tube to be removed.

A tear slipped from her eye despite her best effort
to prevent it. She reached out and took his hand. She
wanted to remain closed off to him forever, but how
could she do that now with him like this? He'd surely
paid a high price for his decisions. No one deserved
the beating he'd endured or the long recovery that lay
ahead of him.

"I'll give you a few minutes," Denise said as she
slipped quietly from the area and left Laura alone.

She pulled up a chair beside his bed and listened to
the hum of the breathing machine. She was still angry,
but she was afraid, too. She'd already lost so much and,
despite her hurt and disillusionment, she wasn't ready
to lose her father, too.

* * *

Laura refused to leave the hospital. In fact, she refused to leave the ICU waiting room even though the hospital's policy would only allow her to visit with her father for fifteen minutes every four hours. But she didn't want to leave in case there was a change in his condition.

She wasn't the only one. Another family also appeared to be camped out in the same area waiting for news. Colton noticed they had blankets and books and snacks. They'd come prepared for a long stay and Colton wished he'd been half as prepared. He would have brought his gun, but the hospital's security measures only allowed sworn officers to carry inside the hospital. Even the security staff wasn't armed. So he'd left his gun locked in his truck in the parking garage. He contemplated going to get it regardless. They were sitting ducks in this waiting room, easy prey for Randall and his men.

He hadn't expected this. He'd known Randall might target Bill Jackson, but to beat him so badly? Logically, it didn't make sense. Bill couldn't repay Randall in this condition, and if Randall thought that nearly killing her father would endear Laura to him, then he was crazier than Colton could have believed.

He took advantage of the lapse of time between visits to phone Detective Merle for an update on the case against Randall. Thankfully, the detective had news.

"Fingerprints found at the scene of the Duncan murder match two of Randall's known associates. We're bringing both men in for questioning."

Finally a break in the case. But Colton knew tying Randall to the attack was still a tricky situation. "Do you think they'll name Randall?"

"I'll do my best to convince them, but it won't be the first time someone has taken the wrap for Randall. He's a charismatic guy and he commands a lot of loyalty from those he employs. Right now, all we have is the ability to place them at the scene of the murder. Hopefully forensics will give us more evidence against them, but we won't get the full results of that for a while."

"Thanks for keeping us updated," Colton told Merle.

"I'll let you know if I come across any new developments."

He hung up and turned to Laura, who was listening intently.

"Nothing," she said, not phrasing it as a question but a statement.

He wished the news was better. He wished he could tell her the cops had Randall dead to rights and he would never bother her again. But he couldn't say that, not yet. He was determined he would and soon. "They're still investigating."

She sighed wearily. "That man thinks he's bulletproof and maybe he is."

"No, Merle seems like a good cop. He'll find something. And he's allowing Blake to go through his files as a backup. He wants to bring down Randall as much as we do."

"No, not as much as me." She turned to look at him and her green eyes reflected fear and sorrow. "It isn't his life on the line if he doesn't."

* * *

The crowd had dispersed and many of her friends had gone home for the night. Several had offered to stay with her, but she'd insisted she was fine. Besides, she had Colton to stay with her and she was confident he wasn't going anywhere. She felt better knowing he was close by. And Denise was right downstairs working a shift in the ER and had promised to check on her during her break.

"Can I get you something?" Colton asked gently.

"I'm fine."

"You need to eat something," he insisted, tilting her chin up to meet his gaze. Honestly, she couldn't remember the last time she'd eaten anything.

"The cafeteria is probably still open. We won't have to be gone long."

"I'm not leaving."

He sighed. "Then how about something from the vending machine? I saw one down the hall by the elevator."

She nodded. "Fine."

She watched him walk down the hall. She wasn't hungry, but he was right about keeping up her strength. He was looking out for her and she needed to remember to show her appreciation more instead of snapping at him.

The phone on the wall rang. Laura knew it was used to alert family members of updates on patients. Her heart lurched. She saw the woman from the other family tense as well, before getting up to answer it. She picked up the phone, then glanced at Laura.

"Family of Bill Jackson?"

Laura sucked in a breath. Why were they calling her? Had her father's condition changed? She stood and the woman held out the phone for her.

Laura took the phone and answered breathlessly. "Yes? Hello? This is Laura Jackson."

"Miss Jackson, Dr. Braxton would like to speak with you about your father's condition. He's waiting for you in room 17 at the end of the hallway." The nurse's voice was curt and to the point.

"Is something wrong?"

"You really need to meet with Dr. Braxton. He's waiting for you now." The click of the phone indicated the nurse had disconnected. Laura hung up the phone and glanced around for Colton, but he wasn't yet back from the snack machines.

Should she wait for him to return? But then, what if Dr. Braxton left? She knew from experience that if she wanted to speak with a doctor, she'd better grab the chance when she had it or he would be gone. It was unusual for physicians to make rounds this late in the day, but it wasn't unheard of. Her mind ticked off all the things that could be wrong. Perhaps her father's blood pressure had dropped or the doctor needed her okay to perform some lifesaving operation?

She approached the woman who had answered the phone. "Would you tell my friend when he returns that I've gone to meet with the doctor?"

She nodded. "Of course."

Laura hurried down the hall. She glanced at the numbers on the door. Room 17 was at the very end and the door was ajar. She pushed it open. The room was dark with the lights off and the curtains drawn.

"Hello? Dr. Braxton?"

She pushed back the curtain blocking half the room and peeked around it.

Something was wrong. Did she have the right room? Hadn't the nurse said room 17? She was certain of it.

Suddenly someone grabbed her from behind and clamped his hand over her mouth, his arms surrounding her. She tried to scream, but the hand over her mouth prevented it.

She'd walked right into a trap.

SIX

Colton fed a dollar through the vending machine money changer, hit the button for a bag of chips, then bent to get it. When he stood again, he saw a man leaning against the doorjamb watching him. The man was tall and dressed in a neat suit and tie. His shoes shone and his hair did, too, from too much grease slicking it back.

Colton tensed. This wasn't just some man waiting to use the vending machine. "Who are you?" he demanded.

The stranger didn't flinch. "I'm here on behalf of Chuck Randall, Mr. Blackwell. I'm here to offer you a deal."

Colton started to reach for his gun, then realized he'd left it in his truck. "What kind of deal?"

The man pulled out an envelope and held it out to Colton. The stranger opened the envelope and Colton saw a large stash of bills. The man flicked his fingers over the bills as if counting them.

"Mr. Randall is prepared to offer you a substantial reward for the return of Laura Jackson. I'm here on his behalf, hoping we can work something out. You see, we know she's here. We could take her by force—"

"You could try," Colton said as menacingly as he could.

"—but we would much rather end this peacefully."

"I cannot be bought. You go back and tell your boss that."

"Mr. Blackwell, we're not looking for a fight here," the man said, "but we are prepared to act if you don't cooperate."

"Again. You can try. You go back and tell your boss that Laura Jackson is under my protection."

"We're also willing to offer you free play in any of Mr. Randall's casinos. That's free for life."

"Not interested," Colton retorted.

He quirked an eyebrow. "Are you sure? That's free gaming for life."

"No. I'm not that guy anymore."

The man set the envelope on the machine, then slowly backed away. "This is just a down payment. There will be more to come. All you have to do is co-operate." He turned and sauntered down the hall to the elevator, then was gone.

Colton stared at the envelope of cash. He fingered the bills and realized it was several thousand dollars. That was a lot of money. Randall thought he could sway Colton with cash or free gaming, but he was wrong.

He stuffed the envelope into his pocket. There might be a way to connect Randall to this cash.

Yet right now he had to get back to Laura. He'd been gone far too long already and didn't want her to worry.

Colton retrieved two sodas and the bag of chips from the vending machine, telling himself he would convince her to at least eat a few chips if nothing else. He hadn't given up on getting her to eat something nutritious, but for the time being it would have to do.

He walked into the waiting room. Laura's spot was empty. He glanced around but didn't see her. A woman in the corner approached him.

"The doctor asked to see her," she told him.

His heart dropped. Had her father's status changed? "Thank you."

He dropped the snacks into an empty chair, then strode through the double doors and approached the nurses' station. "I'm looking for Laura Jackson. She's meeting with Dr. Braxton about her father. Can you tell me where they are?"

The nurse's expression grew confused. "Dr. Braxton isn't on the floor. He was called into an emergency surgery an hour ago. I haven't seen Laura since her last visit with her father."

Fear struck him. He rushed toward Bill Jackson's curtained area and pushed open the curtain. She wasn't there. He ran back into the waiting room.

Oh, God, keep her safe.

He heard a cry for help and spotted the door to the stairs close. He sprinted toward it. In the stairwell, he saw a man pulling Laura with him down the stairs as she fought against him.

"Let her go!" Colton shouted.

The man stopped and looked up at him, then raised his gun toward Colton. Laura screamed and grabbed for it, causing the gun to fire and a bullet to shoot past him. He hurried down the steps as Laura fought the man. Grasping the rails and lurching himself at the guy, Colton kicked the gun from his hand and knocked him against the wall and down several steps. The man scrambled back up the steps for the gun, but Colton reached it first. As he grabbed it, the man turned and took off down the stairs.

Colton's first instinct was to rush after the man, but common sense prevailed. He wasn't leaving Laura again.

"Are you all right?" he asked her.

She gingerly touched a cut on her forehead that was bleeding. "I think I'm okay."

He pushed back her hair and examined the cut. "You may need stitches. I think we should go down to the ER and let them take a look at you."

She agreed without argument.

He glanced at the doorway through which the would-be abductor had fled. The man was surely long gone by now, but that didn't stop him from being cautious. He had the man's gun, though, and he wouldn't hesitate to use it if necessary. "Laura, did you recognize that man?"

She shook her head. "No, I've never seen him before."

"Once we're done in the ER, I want to go check out the hospital security footage. There might be an image of this guy on it that we can use to identify him."

Laura's friend Denise saw them enter the ER and rushed over. "What happened? Are you okay?"

"She was attacked in the stairwell."

Denise checked the wound on her head. "You need stitches. Take her to room 6. I'll do the procedure myself after I finish working up this patient."

Colton helped Laura down the hall and into the room.

"Why don't you go ahead to the security office?" she told him. "I'll be fine here."

No chance. He wasn't leaving her unguarded. He arranged for two security officers to be stationed outside room 6, then phoned Detective Merle, who arrived within a half hour of Colton calling him.

Merle took the assailant's gun, then headed for the security office and Colton joined him. The officer on duty pulled up the video surveillance feeds for the ICU floor. It captured an image of Laura being dragged from a room at the end of the hall and into a stairwell. Colton's blood went cold when he saw the look of terror on her face. If anything had happened to her, he'd have no one to blame but himself.

Taking several deep breaths, he forced himself to calm down. He had a job to do here. Plain and simple. And he wouldn't put Laura at risk by letting his personal feelings mess with his head.

Colton leaned toward the screen, watching intently. Her hands were on the assailant's arms, trying to pull them away, but she was no match for his strength. The security officer cropped the image to show only the man's profile, then emailed it to Detective Merle.

"He was watching out for the camera," Merle said. "He kept his face covered and turned his head. I doubt we'll be able to identify him based on this image. I want images of all the exits. Look for anyone leaving that matches the perpetrator's build and attire."

"I have another idea," Colton said. "There was another man. He approached me at the vending machines. I think he was the diversion."

Merle turned to the video operator. "Pull up images of the vending machines on the ICU floor." He ran through the images within the time frame until Colton came into view.

"There I am."

A moment later the man appeared in the frame.

"That's him."

Colton watched as they spoke for several moments before the stranger handed over the envelope. The man turned to leave and stared right up at the camera. The operator cropped a perfect image of his face.

"He wasn't hiding," Colton said. "He didn't even try to hide his face. He knew the camera was there. He's looking right at it."

"What did he say to you?"

"He offered me money to basically throw Laura to the wolves." He pulled the envelope full of cash out. "I was hoping we could find a way to link this cash to Randall."

Merle examined the cash. "That's unlikely. The bills are out of sequence and small tenders. We may, however, be able to pull some prints from the envelope, but I wouldn't hold your breath about that, either."

"He knew I wouldn't leave Laura for long. He was keeping me busy while his friend lured her down the hall."

Merle made certain he'd received all the images before they left the security office. "Maybe we'll find something that will link this attack to Randall. In the meantime, I want to talk to Laura and take her statement. Stay close."

"I will."

Merle didn't need to worry about that. Colton wasn't leaving her alone again. And as soon as possible, he would get her out of River City and back to the ranch.

Laura didn't complain about the guards Colton had placed at the door. She knew them both and she knew they were necessary. Randall and his men had proved the hospital wasn't a safe place for her. They'd lured her here by beating her father nearly to death, then tried to grab her when she'd come to see him.

Randall had surely hit a new low.

Denise finished stitching her up. "All done. How do you feel?"

"I'm okay," Laura said. She tried to sit up but dizziness washed over her and Denise reached to help her.

"Be careful."

They'd checked her for a concussion, but Laura knew it was only a deep cut. She'd smashed into the railing when the stranger had thrown her aside after Colton's appearance, but she hadn't lost consciousness at all. She shuddered, thinking of what might have happened had he not found her.

But he had. She'd walked into a trap and Colton had rescued her just in time.

Denise shook her head. "I can't believe it's gotten this bad. Why didn't you tell me?"

Laura knew her friend was worried. "I was embarrassed I'd let it go this far. If Colton hadn't been there, I don't know what I would have done."

"He cares for you," Denise said.

"You don't know that."

"I see the way he looks at you. Don't you like him?"

Laura suddenly felt as if she was back in middle school and was getting the lowdown on who liked whom. "Colton is great. He's funny and strong and reliable."

"And gorgeous," Denise finished with a fond smile.

She kept quiet at that remark. It was true she'd found herself unexpectedly attracted to Colton, but Denise knew her history with men. She couldn't allow anything to happen between them.

"Laura, I love you like a sister. You deserve to have someone care for you."

"And I want that. I really do. But you know that's not possible for me. I've put my heart out there too many times only to have it broken. I won't go through that again."

"But maybe this time things could be different."

She wanted to believe in Colton. She owed him so much and he'd been there for her. But it was too frightening to let her heart lead her. She never got the chance to tell her friend that, though, because the door opened and Colton came into the room.

"How are you feeling?" he asked her.

"Better. Denise got me all stitched up and I'm good to go." She looked at her friend. "Right?"

"Yes," Denise said. "Just watch her. Tylenol for any pain. Come back in if you have any nausea or lethargy. You know how this works." She turned to Colton. "Thank you for looking out for my friend," she said, her voice softening.

"My pleasure," he responded.

Denise walked out and closed the door behind her and that was when Laura noticed Detective Merle had come in behind Colton.

"Laura, Detective Merle wants to ask you some questions about the man who tried to attack you."

"Like what kind of questions?"

"Well, for starters, did you recognize the man who grabbed you?" Merle began.

"No. I don't remember seeing him before."

"What about this man? Do you recognize him?" He held out his phone to her and showed her a picture of a dark-haired man in a suit.

"I've never seen him before, either. Who is he?"

"We think he works for Randall. He was in the hospital tonight."

Colton spoke up. "He approached me at the vending machines. We think he was trying to keep me busy while his buddy grabbed you."

She shook her head. "Well, like I said, I've never seen him before."

Merle put away his phone. "Tell me again about the call you received. Was it a man or a woman on the line? Did you recognize the voice?"

She shook her head. "It was a woman's voice. She knew my name. She knew my father's name. She even knew the doctor's name. Do you think it was someone who works at the hospital?"

"Randall has a lot of people indebted to him. Honestly, it could have been anyone. This man who tried to grab you might not even work for Randall. He could have just been looking to collect the money."

She sighed. "Everywhere I go, I'm a target."

"I'll feel better when I get you back home," Colton said.

She nodded, then realized she liked the idea of referring to the ranch as home. It already felt like home to her and she, too, couldn't wait to get back there. "I'll give the ICU nurse your phone number. Denise will also keep me updated on my father's condition. I understand I can't stay here any longer. It's not safe."

Colton nodded. "I'll take you back upstairs to say goodbye, then we'll go." He shook Detective Merle's hand. "Call me if you find out anything else."

"I will," Merle stated.

Colton placed his hand on her back as Laura walked to the elevator. It helped her to keep her balance, knowing he was strong enough to catch her if she stumbled. She felt the nagging pull of a headache coming on and rubbed her face. The local anesthetic must be wearing off and she was about to feel the full force of the gash.

"You okay?" Colton asked as they waited for the doors to open.

"Just a little sore. I'll be better once we're on the road back home."

As they stepped into the elevator, Laura realized

she'd done it, too. She'd referred to Colton's ranch as home and he hadn't flinched when she'd said it.

What would it be like, she wondered, to have a place like the ranch as her home or a man like Colton by her side forever?

She realized such an image warmed her soul.

If only such a scenario could happen, it would be a dream come true.

Laura sat beside her father's bedside and stared at him. He was hooked up to machines that monitored his vitals. Sure, she was angry at him for getting her into such a mess, but that didn't mean she couldn't worry about him. He was still her father and he looked so frail and weak.

She knew he'd been trying. He'd joined Gamblers Anonymous. He'd convinced Colton to act as her protector. Still, he wouldn't have to make up if he hadn't placed her in this situation in the first place by being so weak willed.

All she wanted was a normal life where she got to make her own decisions and she wasn't constantly bombarded with other people's problems. She took things too seriously, she knew. She was too tenderhearted.

Her patient's always seemed to bring that out in her, too, causing her to be constantly stressed. She hadn't yet figured out how to distance herself. In the ER, she saw people who'd been beaten and shot and stabbed…and she longed to help them all. She could help mend their physical wounds, but she longed for more. She longed to help those she saw over and over again realize that it was their own choices that brought them back to the ER again and again. The battered wife she treated at least once every few months who insisted she was only clumsy. The man who kept coming to the ER for alcohol poisoning. As a nurse, she knew one day he wouldn't survive, yet his behavior never changed.

Her coworkers, including Denise, often told her she wasn't cut out to work the ER. That she cared too much and needed to work on a floor where patients were thankful for her kindness. But Laura always seemed to get the ones who wanted to take advantage of her kindness. Give them a smile or a sympathetic ear and she became a target for their emotional blackmail.

Well, she was tired of being manipulated and abused. She would no longer be a victim, either physically or emotionally.

She could love her dad, even pray for him, but she couldn't change his life for him. She stood and wiped the tears that were streaming down her face. Colton had been the one stronghold in all this mess. Her father had asked him to watch over her and she would take solace in his protection.

She kissed her father's cheek, then hurried out of the ICU unit. Colton was in the waiting room and she went straight into his arms, which wrapped comfortably around her. In his embrace, she felt protected and safe. "I'm ready to go," she told him. She stopped herself before she referred to his ranch as home again, but it did already seem like home to her.

Colton kept his arm around her as they took the elevator downstairs, then walked to the parking garage. He'd parked on the third level, so they took another elevator to the floor. As they stepped off the elevator, she caught a glimpse of his truck at the end of a row. She was looking forward to getting on the road and back to the ranch. Funny, she'd never felt as at home even in her own apartment as she did at the ranch.

The sound of tires squealing grabbed her attention. She felt Colton tense and reach for his gun. He didn't have it because it was locked inside his truck.

He gripped her arm and started running to the truck as a car flew down the parking lot ramp and skidded around the corner, barreling toward them. Colton pushed her down and Laura crouched between two parked cars. She looked up in time to see Colton leap onto the hood of another car as the oncoming vehicle slammed into it. Colton fell, sliding to the ground.

"Colton!" He groaned in pain and Laura rushed to him.

His face was red and he was holding his leg and grimacing.

He tried to stand but couldn't. "Help me up," he told her. Laura slipped his arm over her and took on his weight as he climbed carefully to his feet.

He slipped the keys into her hand. "Go to the truck. Get out of here. I'll hold them off."

She glanced at the car and saw two men woozily pouring out after the crash. One had a cut on his head, blood gushing from it. Head wounds notoriously bled and she suspected he would soon show up in the ER for stitches and possibly a concussion. The other was moaning as he emerged from the passenger's side. He was holding his arm tenderly. She wished these men would show up in her ER when she was working. She would show her coworkers just how disconnected she could be.

She ran to the truck and slid behind the wheel, quickly starting it. Colton wanted her to escape, but she wasn't going anywhere without him. Suddenly she remembered the gun locked in the box under the seat. She pulled it out, found the key on the key chain she'd seen him use to secure it and unlocked it, then grabbed the gun. These men didn't know who they were messing with.

The gun was heavy in her hand, much bigger than the one Colton had shown her how to shoot with, but hopefully she wouldn't have to fire it. Her shoulder was still hurting, but she would endure a little pain to rescue Colton.

She jammed the truck into gear and backed out of the spot. Squealing to a stop in front of the wrecked car, she jumped out and pointed the gun toward the two men.

"Don't move," she ordered them. She glanced at Colton. "Get into the truck."

She slid his arm over her shoulder and helped carry his weight as he hobbled toward the truck, but she didn't take her eyes off the two men. Once she opened the side door, Colton crawled inside. She could see he was struggling to keep the pain to himself. His leg might be broken or worse; unfortunately she couldn't examine it here.

She climbed into the front seat and put the truck into gear, yet she couldn't turn off the nurse in her. She motioned to the man with the head wound.

"You'd better get that checked out," she told him. "Looks like you might need stitches."

So maybe her friends were right about her, after all, she thought as she roared out of the parking garage.

"How's your leg?" she asked when they were safely on the highway headed out of River City and Colton had assured her no one was following behind them.

"I think I landed wrong on my knee." He grimaced as he tried to move his leg.

"I should wrap it until we can get it x-rayed. Do you have a first-aid kit in the truck?"

"Under the backseat."

She pulled over to the shoulder and found the kit, removing an ACE bandage to wrap his knee with. Colton opened the passenger door, then hung his leg out as Laura bandaged it.

"When we get to Compton, we should go right to the medical center and have it examined. You could have torn ligaments."

She glanced up at him and saw him staring at her. "You were amazing back there," he told her. "I think you really put the fear into those guys. I know I was certainly scared of you."

She grinned at his wit. He was teasing her again, which meant either the pain was becoming manageable or he'd simply found a way through it.

"Thankfully, I didn't have to fire. If I had, they would have known for certain I had no idea what I was doing."

"You could've taken out those boys."

She flashed another smile, happy to know he had so

much confidence in her. "Really? You think I could've hit them?"

"Sure, they're much bigger than an aluminum can."

He reached out and gently stroked her cheek. And suddenly the lightheartedness of the moment morphed into something much more intense. He brushed her lips with the pad of his thumb and she knew he wanted more than a touch of skin against lips. She wanted it, too. He pulled her to him and kissed her, softly at first, then more intensely. She melted into his embrace, loving the feeling of his arms wrapped protectively around her. She could live in his embrace forever and she realized she wanted to. She wanted to call the ranch her home without feeling guilty about it and she could imagine building a life with this man.

But she pushed away from him instead and an onslaught of emotions overwhelmed her. She'd lost so much already and it pained her to think of losing Colton, too, but she was still so afraid of trusting him completely.

She was so afraid of being disappointed by love again.

Colton left the Compton Medical Center with a knee brace and a set of crutches. According to the X-rays, he'd merely stretched several ligaments in his knee. It hurt like crazy, but at least nothing was broken or torn.

He let Laura drive to the ranch, but he watched her all the while keeping one eye looking over their shoulder in case they were being followed. He tried to figure out what was going on inside that beautiful head of hers. She'd been different after they'd shared a kiss.

She'd pulled away from him not only physically but emotionally, too, and he had no idea why.

Maybe it was just all too much for her, he thought. He hoped that was all it was. She'd been through a lot with her father's beating and Randall's attacks. He hoped she would be better once they reached the ranch. Yet he had to keep reminding himself that her stay with him was temporary. He'd already fallen for her spunk and her determination, and while he sensed Laura shared his attraction, he knew his past was something he couldn't run from…something she could never accept.

She parked in front of the house, then helped him inside and into his recliner, waiting on him like the nurturer she was, fixing him a large glass of iced tea along with an ice pack for his knee. She even tried to convince him to take the pain medicine the hospital doctor had provided, but he waved it off. His knee might be out of commission, but he still wanted to keep his mind as sharp as possible and his gun within reach.

"We're quite a pair, aren't we?" she asked, settling into the couch. "You with your knee. Me with my stitches."

He wondered if she was losing hope in him. "Just a setback," he told her. "It happens. Our bodies will mend. I'll be back up on my feet by tomorrow, I'm sure."

"That knee needs more than a few hours to mend itself. Do you always have to push the limits like that?"

He shrugged. "I do what I need to do."

"How are you keeping it together, Colton? After all that's happened, you seem so grounded. I'm going crazy with worry about everything, but you remain so calm under pressure. What's your secret? Did you learn that from being a ranger?"

"Partly, I guess I did. But mostly it's just about having faith."

She sighed. "I try. I really do, but sometimes I just get so scared. I have to admit I don't see God working in all of this."

"But He is, Laura. Really He is. Have you ever heard the story from the Bible of Daniel in the lions' den?"

"Of course. Anyone who's been in Sunday school has heard that story."

"I saw this painting once depicting that scene. In the painting, Daniel had his back to the lions and his hands were clasped behind him. He was staring up as if he didn't have a care in the world, but there in the background was a line of hungry beasts waiting to devour him." He spoke softly, his gaze never leaving hers. "I confess I sometimes feel like Daniel in the lions' den. I live in a world where lions are watching my every move, waiting for permission to devour me. The only thing that stops them is God.

"That's how it was in that painting and I believe that's how it is in life, as well. I want to have the same faith that Daniel had. He trusted God enough to turn his back on those lions and not fear them at all. Can you imagine the kind of freedom trusting in God that much would have?"

She stared at him with sad, green eyes that looked defeated and he prayed she wasn't losing hope.

"It's been a long day," she said. "I think I'll turn in. Do you need anything before I go upstairs?"

"No, I'm good."

Once he heard the bedroom door shut, he knocked the ice pack from his leg, then pushed himself to his feet. He wanted nothing more at that moment than to remain in the recliner all night. It wouldn't be the first time he'd slept there. But he had something else he had to do before he could sleep. He grabbed the crutches and made his way slowly into the laundry room to his weapons closet, where he pulled out two handguns. He made sure they were loaded before he carried them carefully back to the den.

With his weapons by his sides and Laura safely upstairs, he closed his eyes and drifted into sleep.

Laura jumped up in bed, pulled awake by a terrifying dream. She'd been the one in the lions' den. The hungry lions had been teasing her, chasing her, watching and waiting for their moment to pounce. Colton had been there with her, a warrior swinging his sword to try to protect her, but she'd known he was no match for the horde of beasts. She'd awoken before the animals attacked, but it had been a horrific dream and her heart was still racing.

She pulled back the covers and padded into the bathroom for some water to calm her parched throat. Why did a dream have such an effect on her?

She remembered Colton talking about how God had kept the lions away from Daniel, how He'd closed the mouths of the beasts.

Right now, she could relate to the story. Like Daniel, she had lions circling her, waiting to pounce. Was her brain trying to ease her into the recognition that she was doomed to be devoured by the lions swarming around her?

She walked back into the bedroom and set her water on the nightstand. On the bottom shelf, she spotted the Bible Colton kept there. She thought about the story in Daniel. God had sent His angel to close the mouths of the lions. If God had sent her Colton, then why was she dreaming that he couldn't protect her? She had become so used to men letting her down that she'd unconsciously decided that Colton would, too. Only God could have closed those lions' mouths. Would He do the same for her? Or was she destined to be let down by God just as she had been by every other person in her life?

Colton woke to the intermingling smells of coffee, biscuits and bacon. His mouth was watering before he even opened his eyes. When he did, he noticed a blanket over him and knew Laura must have covered him with it while he'd slept.

So much for no one being able to sneak up on him.

He got up and noticed his knee didn't pain him nearly as badly this morning as it had last night. That was good. He needed to be mobile again as soon as possible. He couldn't protect Laura from Randall from his spot in the recliner.

He poured himself a cup of coffee, then walked outside. Laura was curled up in the rocker, a blanket wrapped around her and a cup of coffee in her hand. Milo, as usual, sat at her feet.

"Morning," he said and she smiled up at him.

"Good morning. How did you sleep?"

He set down his coffee, then lowered himself into the second rocker, careful to keep his knee straight. "Good. Real good, actually. I don't even remember you coming downstairs, much less making breakfast."

"Well, I tried not to wake you."

"I don't usually sleep so hard," he said.

"Well, you needed it. I'm not sorry."

"What did you do?" he asked her, realizing she was not apologizing for nothing.

"I drugged your iced tea."

"You did *what*? Are you insane?" A muscle ticked in his jaw as he glared at her. "What if someone had tried to get into the house last night? I was dead to the world."

"But that didn't happen," she pointed out. "Besides, I only gave you half a dose of your prescribed medication. And it helped. Admit it, you feel better."

He wanted to stay angry with her, but he had to admit he did feel better. Still, he wasn't going to let her off the hook that easily. "Do you drug all your patients?" he asked her sarcastically.

"No, but I should. I think life would be much more peaceful." She flashed him a coy smile that let him know she was only joking. But then her demeanor turned more serious. "You know, I've been sitting out here this morning watching the sunrise and listening to the birds and the sounds of nature, and I realized I want this. I want a more peaceful life, a slower pace. I've been working in the ER at River City Medical Center for years and the grind is hectic." She blew out a breath.

"Maybe my friend Denise is right. I'm not really cut out to handle the fast pace of the ER. I want to take care of my patients, not get them in and out as quickly and as efficiently as possible."

His heart soared. Was she saying she wanted to stay here? With him? For good? He took a long, slow sip of his coffee before he spoke just to make sure this excited hopefulness he felt didn't show. "I'm sure Compton Med is always looking for qualified nurses. And don't worry, I won't tell them you drugged me." He gave her a wink and she smiled.

He remembered the weight of Laura in his arms and the lovely scent of her. He couldn't deny it any longer. This auburn-haired beauty had reeled him in like a fish on a hook. He could already imagine a life with her here on the ranch. Could see her cooking for their family or helping around the ranch. She said she loved the beauty and peacefulness of the place, but was it enough—was *he* enough—to give her the life she dreamed of?

Laura fixed Colton a plate of eggs with bacon and a biscuit. She'd enjoyed making breakfast for him. Enjoyed waking up early, watching the sunrise from the rocker on the porch, listening to the peaceful sounds of the morning on the ranch. And she'd meant what she'd said to him about being ready for a slower pace of life. Compton—and Colton—seemed to offer that.

But as she carried him a breakfast plate, she realized she was making plans that might not even matter. The content of her dream was still with her. She hadn't been able to go back to sleep, fearful of seeing the ending, of witnessing those lions roaring at them.

She instinctively shuddered at the thought and Colton noticed.

"Are you cold? The mornings here can get pretty chilly, although not usually this early in the year."

"I'm not cold. I was just remembering a dream from last night."

"Do you want to tell me about it?"

She recounted the dream, the lions roaring and Colton holding them back with a sword. He listened intently, and when she was through, she watched him, waiting for him to tell her that she was crazy to let a dream affect her so.

He didn't say that. Instead he took another sip of his coffee. "Did you actually see us being killed?"

"No. I awoke before that happened, but I know it did happen. I *felt* it. I don't think it's a sign of anything… It just disturbed me."

"It is a sign," he told her gently. "It's a sign that you're afraid. I'm not surprised. But what you saw in your dream was me doing battle with a sword. The Bible calls God's word a sword of truth. Maybe that's what I was yielding."

"But you were killed in my dream."

"No, I wasn't, darlin'. That was only your fear surfacing. You never saw us killed because it didn't happen. You're scared and that's understandable." He stood and reached for her hand, then put his arms around her. "I won't let anything happen to you. Regardless of some dream you had, God brought you to me, Laura. He doesn't have you in that lions' den alone. He's fighting for you…and so am I."

She rested her head against his chest and listened to the steady thump of his heartbeat. Those were the very words of comfort she'd needed to hear. He tightened his arms around her and she felt safe and protected. However she had gotten here, she was glad she'd come. She was glad she'd let Colton into her life. And mostly, she was glad he'd managed to find a way to sneak into her guarded heart.

SEVEN

Just because he had an injured leg didn't mean the work on the ranch ended. Colton called Tony and gave his apologies. Tony accepted them and said he understood, but Colton could tell he was still miffed, yet he needed to work. Colton authorized him to hire an additional worker to take up Colton's slack for the next few days.

Once that was taken care of, he noticed he had a missed a call from Detective Merle. He phoned him back and was surprised by Merle's request.

"I need you to come to town. I have something I need you and Laura to see."

He grimaced, but not from the pain in his knee as much as from the idea of taking Laura to River City. "I'd rather not take her back there. Isn't this something you can tell me over the phone?"

"No. You really need to come. It's important."

"Fine, but I'm not bringing Laura." He figured he could sneak in and out of town without anyone knowing. But he knew Laura pretty well by now and if she knew where he was going, she would insist on coming. He couldn't allow that. She was an open target in that town. At least here he could offer her some form of security.

But she would still need to be protected even while he was gone. He dialed Blake's number, and when his friend answered, he had a big favor to ask.

"I need you to convince Miranda to invite Laura over this afternoon."

He explained the situation to Blake. His friend wanted to accompany him as well, but Colton convinced him that he needed him to protect Laura.

Blake finally agreed to help. "I told Miranda I would come by this afternoon and do some work on her car that I've been promising to do. Why don't I have Laura come with me?"

"That sounds perfect. Thanks, Blake."

"Where are you going to tell her you're going?"

"I'll say I need to pick up some supplies for the ranch. I'll only be gone a few hours."

He hung up the phone, then went inside to tell Laura about the invitation to Miranda's. She wouldn't be happy when she found out the truth about where he'd been, but he knew he was doing the right thing. He needed to return to River City and he just couldn't risk her safety by having her accompany him.

Detective Merle had instructed Colton to park in the back lot. He met him at the rear entrance to the police station, then had Colton follow him down an empty hallway.

"What's with the cloak and dagger?" Colton asked him. He'd wondered all the way here what the big news was that the detective had been unable to share over the phone, and he had to admit his curiosity was peaked. He hoped it was good news. It would be great to have something positive to share with Laura.

"You'll see." Merle walked down the hall and opened a door, ushering him through.

Inside the room was a man Colton recognized as one of Randall's henchmen—the man from the vending machine, right down to his slicked-back dark hair and impressive suit. "What's he doing here?" Colton asked.

His mind immediately assumed the worst. Had Merle led him into a trap? Was he on Randall's payroll, after all? Suddenly he was thankful he'd left Laura back in Compton.

Merle closed the door. "I'd like you to meet—"

"I know who he is," Colton stated coldly. "He works for Randall."

Merle smirked. "Not quite. His name is Joe Knox. Agent Joe Knox of the FBI."

Agent Knox greeted him with a nod. "I know this comes as a surprise to you. I managed to infiltrate Randall's organization eighteen months ago. I've been gathering and documenting his illegal activities in the hope of building a case against him."

Suddenly the picture-perfect photo of his face via the hospital security cameras made sense. He'd wanted Merle to look into his identity. But then Colton remembered Knox had been a decoy and anger rushed through him.

"You plotted to abduct Laura Jackson. You kept me busy while your friend grabbed her. And you stood around while they beat her father nearly to death. Or were you in on that, too?"

"I had nothing to do with that or with the death of her neighbor," the fed insisted. "I only found out about those things after the fact. And, yes, Randall ordered the assaults. The men who killed the old lady went too far. They weren't there to kill her, only to get information from her about where Laura was hiding."

Colton stared at the undercover agent. He was inclined to believe what Knox was saying, but he still needed answers. "Why are you telling me all this now?"

"Because Randall knows about the investigation. My cover is still intact for the time being, but he knows the FBI is gathering evidence to bring him down. He's knows he's about to be indicted. His days are numbered and he's angry. He's striking out at anything and anyone he can…and right now Laura is his prime target."

"And because he's got nothing to lose, he just got more dangerous," Colton finished.

"That's right. I've been keeping this case very private to avoid leaks, but after the Duncan murder, I knew I had to speak out, to warn you in some way." He cleared his throat. "I heard Detective Merle was the lead investigator on the case and I knew he was one of the few River City police not on Randall's payroll. I had to get permission from my handler to break my cover to tell you this, but I thought it was important. Of course, if this in any way jeopardizes my case against Randall, it would be the end of my career."

"Don't worry. We'll keep your secret." Colton reached

out and shook the man's hand. "Thank you for coming forward."

Knox shook his hand. "Keep her safe."

"I will," Colton assured him.

As he left the police station and headed back to Compton, relief flowed over him. Learning the FBI was closing in on Randall was good news for Laura. If Randall's days of freedom were numbered, then so were Laura's days of living in fear of him. He couldn't wait to tell her.

It was already dark outside and he was sleeping when his phone rang. He glanced at the caller ID before answering. It was his neighbor to the east and that put Colton on alert. It was too late for a friendly phone call. "Hello, Mr. Sheppard. What can I do for you?"

"I see smoke coming from your back pasture, Colton. I think it's a grass fire."

He hurried to the window and peered out to the east. Sure enough, he saw smoke billowing up over the barn.

"I'll call the volunteer fire department, then meet you out there to help."

"Thanks, Mr. Sheppard."

He hung up the phone. They'd had an excessively dry summer and hadn't seen rain in months, so he knew any spark could have started a fire and it could spread quickly out of control. But how had it started? He hadn't noticed any lightning that could have hit and that pasture was too far off the road for a passing car to toss a cigarette out the window. Regardless of how it had started, he needed that pastureland and he also needed to keep the fire from spreading to the rest of his farm. He pulled on his boots and a shirt.

If he didn't get this fire under control, he might not have a ranch left.

Laura awoke to the sound of the dogs barking. She heard the sound of boots clunking against the wooden porch. A bright light caught her gaze through the window and she looked out to see a figure heading for the shop with a flashlight.

She rushed downstairs and saw Colton wasn't there. That must have been him she'd seen through the window.

A moment later she heard the roar of an ATV engine as it approached the house. She stepped outside as Colton stopped in front.

"There's a brush fire in the pasture. I have to go check on my cattle and try to contain the fire."

"How can I help?" she asked.

"Stay inside and set the alarm. I'll be back as soon as I can." He took off on the ATV toward the smoke now visible in the distance.

Laura hurried back inside wondering if she should call someone for help. Perhaps Blake would come and lend a hand. Did the fire department respond to pasture fires out this far? She didn't know but thought she should try.

She phoned Blake's number first, then listened as he answered, his voice groggy with sleep. When Laura explained about the fire, his voice cleared. "I'm on my way. Are you all right there alone?"

"Yes, I'm fine. I'm just worried about the fire."

"Don't worry. We have an excellent volunteer fire department. I'll phone them on my way there."

Laura thanked him, then hung up.

She keyed in the alarm code, then stepped onto the porch, noticing the wind had picked up. Dry weather and wind were a disastrous combination when it came to fire. The sound of dogs barking in the distance reached her ears. They must have followed Colton to the scene. Hopefully they would stay back and safe. She hoped Colton stayed safe, too, but she instinctively knew he would do whatever he had to to save his ranch.

It would be hard to relax until she knew the outcome, but she went back inside. Then she saw Colton's Bible on the table and placed her hand atop it, noticing the smooth feel of the leather. Although it had been quite a long time since she'd prayed, she did now, praying fervently for Colton and whoever arrived to help him. She prayed for their safety and for the land to be preserved and realized her anxiety over the situation was already dissipating.

Her head jerked up when she heard the creak of the back door opening. Colton was in the field…so who was entering the house?

She moved as quietly as a mouse toward the kitchen, where she could get a better glance at the back door. She was probably overreacting. Was it Blake coming to help with the fire or Miranda stopping by to keep her company? But she hadn't heard a vehicle approaching, so she knew it couldn't be either of them.

Laura leaned over the kitchen island and saw the back door slowly opening. She held her breath, trying to convince herself she was only letting her imagination run wild. That it had been the wind or one of the dogs pushing open a door left ajar.

But then a figure appeared in the mudroom.

Her heart thundering in her ears, she crouched behind the island and peeked out. The man was dressed all in black, his face shadowed beneath a ball cap and the lack of light. She should have hit the overhead switch. That might have spooked him, frightened him off long enough for Colton to return.

She sucked in a breath as the realization hit her. This had all been a ploy to get Colton out of the house and away from her. This man had probably set the very fire that was now raging outside.

He'd made plans to get rid of Colton so he could get to her. Laura shivered with fear. But who was he?

She had to get out of there and to the safety of others. Had to find Colton. She rushed for the front door but froze when she heard footsteps outside the door and saw the jiggle of the handle.

The back-door intruder rushed toward her and Laura turned and ran up the steps, locking herself into her bedroom. She picked up the cordless phone and quickly dialed Colton's number. It rang and rang, then went to voice mail. She quickly hung up and dialed Blake's number. His phone also went straight to voice mail. Were they so focused on fighting the fire that they didn't hear their phones? She quickly dialed 9-1-1 instead.

"There are two intruders inside the house at the Blackwell ranch," she told the operator in a hushed voice. "Please send help."

The bedroom doorknob jiggled and Laura knew they were trying to get into her room.

"They're here," she whispered into the phone.

The operator responded calmly. "I've alerted the sheriff's office, but Dispatch says it may take a while. Most of the on-duty officers are responding to a fire."

"I know. I think that was a diversion."

They tried the door again and she knew it was only a matter of time before they got through.

She had to get out of there.

She pulled open the window.

"Stay on the line with me," the operator said. "Tell me what's happening."

"I have to get out. I'm going out the window." She pulled out the emergency ladder stowed under the bed, hooked it on the windowsill, then tossed it out. She knew if she could get out and go around the house, she could probably get to the weapons closet before the men realized she was gone. She started down the ladder. The phone slipped from her hand and hit the ground. She hurried down and picked it up, seeing the screen was cracked and the metal backing was separated.

"Hello? Hello?"

The operator did not respond. Laura tried dialing again, but nothing happened. The phone was broken.

She dropped it and looked up at the house. She heard the bedroom door burst open through the raised window and the two men talking about finding her. Laura ran around the house and slowly opened the back door, hating the way it cringed. She'd been glad for it earlier, but now hoped it wouldn't alert her intruders to her presence.

One of them came around the outside of the house before Laura could get inside to reach the weapons closet. "There she is!" he hollered.

She turned and jumped off the steps, then ran from the house as fast as she could. She had to get to Colton or find someone to help her. His truck was parked by the barn, but she didn't have the keys. Then she remembered the gun under his seat. She crawled into the truck and slid across the seat, feeling underneath it for the gun, but she felt nothing. It wasn't there. He must have removed it.

Laura got out of the truck. She had no keys and no weapons. But even though she couldn't improvise keys, she could find a weapon. She ran into the barn and grabbed a pitchfork used to bale hay. When she heard the men outside, she quickly hid, crouching in the corner of an empty stall.

The old door groaned open and Laura held her breath, praying it was the wind. She heard hard steps against the wooden floor and knew they'd found her. Clutching the pitchfork in her hand, she was poised and ready to strike.

"Gotcha!" one man exclaimed as his big hands reached in to grab her. She saw his face and realized it was one of the McGowen cousins who had broken into the house before and tried to abduct her.

Laura screamed, raised the fork and jammed it into him. She felt his flesh tear against the sharp metal. He cried out, then pulled the weapon from her hand and slung it across the barn.

He grabbed her arm and dragged her outside, Laura kicking and screaming the entire time.

"Leave me alone!" she shrieked. "You'll have to kill me before I'll willingly go with you."

The other McGowen raised his shirt to reveal a gun. "Oh, you'll come willingly or I'll have to use this. I'm not supposed to kill you, but I think I'll still get paid if I suddenly develop a hair trigger."

"Please," Laura pleaded. "You don't know what he'll do to me."

He shook his head. "Lady, that's not our problem."

Laura heard the cock of a gun and they all turned. Colton was standing with a rifle raised at them.

"No, but *this* is your problem," he stated in a deceptively calm tone. "Let her go."

The one holding her tightened his grip. "There's only one of you. There're two of us."

"You need to learn to count," Colton told him as Blake appeared from the opposite side, a rifle trained on the two men.

"The McGowen cousins," Blake said. "And which one of you scum hit my fiancée?"

The man loosened his hold on Laura and she slipped from his grasp and ran to Colton, stepping behind him.

"Throw down your weapons and put your hands on your heads," Blake demanded and the two men complied, tossing their guns away.

Blake approached them while Colton continued to keep him covered with the rifle. Only when both men were handcuffed did Laura see Colton lower the rifle and feel his muscles begin to relax.

He turned and pulled her into a hug, kissing her long and hard, his embrace full of fear and grateful relief. "I came back as soon as I realized the fire was a diversion. I thought I'd lost you," he whispered, his voice hoarse.

"You didn't," she assured him. "I knew you'd come for me." And she had. She'd known it deep down in her soul.

His hand stroked her cheek. "I'll always come for you, Laura. You can trust that."

She leaned into his embrace and felt at home for the first time in a very long time.

Colton, along with Blake, members of the volunteer fire department and several neighbors, battled the fire for several hours before finally putting it out. Laura did what she could to help, offering water to drink to those who needed it and tending to several minor burns sustained fighting the blaze. Another deputy had taken the McGowen cousins and booked them into the jail.

Around 4:00 a.m., the fire was finally out and the crowd of men who'd rushed to help dispersed. The air was heavy with the smell of burned grass and Laura hated to see what that patch of field would look like in the light of day. She wouldn't have to wait long. The sun would be up in less than two hours.

Colton drove them back to the house and she watched him walk toward the porch, limping on his injured leg and just plain worn down from fighting the fire for hours. Things had changed between them. Laura felt it and she was certain he did, too. She was comfortable here at the ranch with him and she'd never felt she belonged anywhere the way she did here.

She went into the house but didn't see Colton. She checked the living room, thinking he might be asleep on the couch. He wasn't, so she looked around for him and found him passed out upstairs in his own bed. He'd been so tired, he forgot he'd been sleeping on the pull-out sofa downstairs. She pulled the blanket over him, then left him alone to sleep. She knew he needed it.

Laura was folding towels when a car pulled up to the house. She tensed for a moment and checked to make sure the alarm was set and Colton's gun was within reach on the end table.

She peeked through the curtain and saw Miranda stepping onto the porch.

Laura felt silly at the way her mind reacted. She'd become so accustomed to being on the lookout that she now expected an attack around every corner. She clicked off the alarm and opened the door to greet Miranda.

"Hi, there. I wasn't expecting you. Come inside."

Miranda walked in and glanced around. "Where's Colton?"

"Upstairs sleeping. He was up all night fighting the fire. I know Blake was, too, so will you thank him for me when you see him?"

She nodded and Laura noticed her friend seemed distracted.

"Is something wrong?" Laura asked her.

Miranda was quick to respond. "No, not really. It's

just…" She shook her head, reluctant to speak. "Never mind. It's nothing."

Laura didn't believe her. Miranda hadn't driven all the way over here for nothing. And her friend seemed anxious. She wasn't the same happy person Laura had come to know.

"It's not nothing, Miranda. Something obviously has you flustered."

"I guess I am. I have a dilemma and I don't know quite what to do about it."

"Would you like to talk about it? Sometimes it helps to share with another person. Is it about Blake?"

"No, no. Blake and I are fine. Although he did tell me something that just doesn't sit right with me. Laura, this may be none of my business, but I feel like we've become friends and I don't think it's right to keep this secret from you."

"Well, I appreciate the thought, Miranda, but if Blake wants to keep something from me—"

"It's not Blake's secret. It's Colton's."

Laura immediately felt her stomach knot. "Colton is keeping something secret from me?"

"It's about his past. When I told you before that Colton was in rehab, I think you misunderstood. He wasn't injured in the ambush. In fact, he was the only one of them not to be seriously injured. But I guess they all had their ways of coping. Colton started gambling."

"Gambling?" Hot tears pulled at her eyes. No, it couldn't be true. *Oh, God, please don't let this be true.*

"It got quite bad. Blake and the other rangers staged an intervention and got him help. But, given your current situation, I guess he thought keeping that from you was best. I disagree. Maybe it's not my place to tell you, but I think us girls should stick together, don't you?"

She managed to nod. Yes, she was thankful for Miranda's honesty. She was also angry. Angry at Colton for keeping such a secret from her. Her mind swam with confusion. This was just like her father all over again.

"There's something else."

Laura closed her eyes and tried to breathe. How much more could she handle?

"Blake thinks Colton might be gambling again."

Laura's heart dropped. It was her worst fear coming true. It couldn't be. Colton wouldn't let her down this way. She couldn't fathom it.

"Why does he think that?"

"He said Colton has been going to River City on a regular basis now for months. He went again just yesterday while you were at my house. Blake believes that's how he knew about you and your situation."

It made sense. He never had truly explained how he and her father had met. Had they connected at the gaming tables?

"Blake also told me Colton's gotten behind on his mortgage on this ranch. He might lose it. I'm really worried about him, but I'm worried about you, too, Laura. I think we've become friends and now I think this affects you, as well."

Laura felt physically ill at the prospect that what Miranda was saying might be true. She put her head in her hands. This couldn't be happening to her, not again.

Miranda placed a hand over hers, her face full of

concern. "I still think Colton is a great guy and I can see he adores you." She frowned. "I shouldn't have said anything."

"No, I'm glad you did." She hugged Miranda, thankful for such a good friend. "I don't know what I'm going to do," she said. "How can I trust him to keep me safe if he's constantly thinking about his next score?"

"There is one alternative. If you don't feel safe here anymore, you could come stay with me. No one would know you were there and I'm sure I can convince Blake to station some officers around to keep an eye on the place."

"I appreciate the offer. I just don't know yet." It didn't feel right…what Miranda was saying. It didn't feel right not believing in Colton. She needed to talk to him about this and find out for herself if it was true.

Colton jerked awake. It was daylight outside the window and he suddenly realized he'd fallen asleep and left Laura alone after returning from the fire. He jumped off the bed and hurried downstairs, praying she was okay and nothing had happened while he was sleeping.

He found her in the kitchen intently concentrating on scrubbing a pan in the sink. "Laura, what a relief!" As he came up beside her, his heart returned to a steady beat. "I had an awful fright when I awoke and realized I'd left you unguarded. The McGowens might be in jail, but we don't know for sure they were behind all the attacks."

She stopped scrubbing for only a moment but didn't look at him. "I'm fine." She continued scrubbing.

He walked over to the kitchen counter and poured himself a cup of cold coffee. "We were fortunate. The blaze could have spread to the house and barn. Thankfully, the wind wasn't blowing strong last night. I guess God was looking out for us."

"I guess He was."

Colton looked at the pan, knowing neither of them had cooked anything that would have resulted in a mess big enough for the intensity with which she was scrubbing. "Are you okay?"

"I'm fine," she said in a monotone that indicated she was anything but fine. She sounded angry. Angry with him. But he hadn't done anything to elicit such ire unless she was upset that he'd fallen asleep on her.

"Did I do something to upset you?"

She dropped the pan, then towel-dried her hands as she glared at him. "I don't know, Colton. Did you do something? Is there anything that you've been keeping from me? That you were hiding about yourself that you didn't want me to know?"

Her accusation caught him completely off guard. He gulped, nervous at what she might be talking about. This might be worse than he'd thought. But how could she know about his past? He decided it was time she knew the truth. The whole truth about Colton Blackwell.

"You found out about my past, about my gambling?"

Her silence only confirmed what he already knew. Anger glowed from her eyes along with an uncertainty about him that broke his heart.

"I'm not that guy anymore, Laura. I left him behind me quite a while ago. I promise you I've changed."

"I've heard that promise too many times before, Colton, and it's always turned out to be an empty promise." The ice in her voice was nearly more than he could stand.

He knew his past wasn't something he could put on the back burner and forget. It was a part of him. A man didn't change right away and he couldn't expect anyone to accept that he'd changed. Trust was a delicate thing and he'd rambled over his friends' faith in him like a train racing down a track. He'd known from the start that regaining trust would take time, a lot of time, and he'd readied himself to face it, to persevere. Of course, his friends had given him a lot of leeway. They all believed in him. He hoped she could, too.

He set down his cup and looked her eye to eye. "You've never heard it from me, Laura."

"Did you go to River City yesterday while I was at Miranda's?"

"Who told you that? Let me explain."

She shook her head and her expression was one of disgust. "How can I believe you? How can I ever believe you again? You lied to me."

"Would you have come here with me or stayed here with me if you'd known? No, you would have walked right out that door and into the hands of Chuck Randall. I was looking out for you."

"You were looking out for yourself," she shot back. "I can't believe I trusted you." Tears pooled in her beautiful green eyes. "That's the worst part, Colton. I thought you were different. I thought finally I had met a man who wouldn't let me down." They spilled out onto her cheeks and she wiped them away. "I was wrong. You're just like every other man I've ever met." She ran up the stairs. The slamming of the bedroom door pierced his heart as surely as her final words had.

Bitter emotion threatened to knock him off his feet. Some part of him knew he should have been straight with her from the start, but his logical mind said his honesty would only have put her life in danger.

He'd had a job to do to keep her safe and he'd used whatever means necessary to do so. If she didn't like him now, so be it. He'd always known she was too good for him. He'd told himself from the start that he couldn't have her. Only his own foolish desire had tricked him into actually believing she could ever love someone like him.

He fell into a chair and put his hands over his face. He just hadn't realized it would hurt this badly when cold reality set in.

She ran upstairs to gather her things, her heart breaking as she realized all she was losing. She certainly couldn't depend on Colton to keep her safe now. He'd betrayed her and she needed to get away from him.

She locked the door and picked up the phone, dialing Miranda's number.

"I can't stay here anymore. I'm not safe here," she said when Miranda answered. "Is that offer to stay with you still open?"

"Of course, honey. I'll be right over to get you."

"Thank you, Miranda." She choked back a sob. "I don't know what I would do without a friend like you."

She hung up, then packed her things. She was thankful to have found a good friend like Miranda. Experience had taught her that men couldn't be trusted and that seemed to be proving true for her once again. People didn't change. The men she let into her life would always let her down.

EIGHT

Colton went out to feed the livestock. As he was coming out of the barn, he saw Miranda's car drive away but didn't think anything of it until he returned to the house to find Laura missing.

He called her name, but she didn't answer and his worry meter edged up a notch. Why wasn't she answering him? Was there a reason she couldn't?

He pulled his gun, then moved around the house, searching and clearing each area as he went. When he reached her bedroom, she wasn't there, but he did notice her suitcase was gone from the bench where she'd placed it. He pulled open the drawers, but her things were gone.

It was clear she hadn't been forced to leave. That explained seeing Miranda's car pulling away so quickly.

He put away his gun and pulled out his phone, dialing Miranda's number. No response. He dialed Blake's and his friend answered quickly.

"I'm trying to reach Miranda. Have you spoken to her?"

"No, not today. Why?"

"I'm pretty sure Laura just left me and I think she's with Miranda."

Blake sighed. "I'm afraid that's the least of your concerns today. I just got word that Joe Knox is dead. They pulled his body out of the river an hour ago."

"He's dead?" Fear ripped through Colton. If Knox's cover had been blown, as it surely had been, then Laura was still in danger from Randall. They would have to find another way out of this mess.

"It gets worse," Blake continued. "Chuck Randall is gone. FBI agents raided his home and his business and he wasn't at either. His whereabouts are currently unknown."

Colton's heart dropped. Randall was on the run. He was now truly a caged lion on the prowl. But did he still have Laura in his sights?

Aside from the fear that ate at him over Randall's unknown location, he was also devastated that Laura had left. It didn't matter that he told himself he could never have her or that he had no right to fall for her, the truth was that he *had* fallen for her. And if anything happened to her because she'd left his protection, because she'd found out about his past and run, it would ruin him.

She had to be at Miranda's, and it made him mad that she didn't trust him, but also that she would place herself in a situation where she wasn't fully protected. He needed to confront her face-to-face, to remind her of the danger she was still in and to somehow convince her this was all just a big misunderstanding and that she needed to return with him. He grabbed his keys and got into his truck.

He sped across town and roared into Miranda's driveway, then pounded on her door. She might not want to answer his calls, but he was determined he wasn't leaving until she opened the door.

Thankfully, he didn't have to make that demand. Miranda opened the door after his first knock.

"Where's Laura?" he demanded.

Miranda stood firm, her chin raised stubbornly, clearly determined to stand up for her friend. "She's here, but she's upstairs resting."

"I just need to speak to her, Miranda."

"She doesn't want to see you, Colton."

"Her life is in danger. I need to see her."

"It's okay, Miranda." He heard Laura's voice and looked up to see her listening on the steps. She walked down. "I'll talk to him. It's fine."

Miranda shrugged and stepped aside, but Colton noticed neither woman invited him inside. That was fine with him. He'd stay outside if he needed to, as long as Laura listened to what he had to say.

She stared at him, her eyes cold and her arms folded defiantly across her chest. "Whatever excuse you've come up with, I've already heard it all before."

"Whatever you think happened isn't true. You remember that man who approached me at the hospital? He turned out to be an undercover FBI agent. I went to River City to meet with him. I know I should have told you, but I didn't want you going back there. He was trying to contact me to let me know that the FBI is preparing to arrest Randall. He wanted to warn me to look out for him."

Anger burned on her cheeks and in her eyes. She was hurt. She truly believed in her heart that she'd been betrayed. But she had no clue that he would never betray her. He would do anything to keep her safe...even if it meant letting her go.

"It was all a ruse, Laura. You have to trust me. It was all just a ruse to keep you safe."

She shook her head and rubbed her temple as if trying to hold back a headache. "I can't do it again, Colton. I've already been through this back and forth before with my father. I vowed I would never let my guard down again. I don't know if what you're telling me is true or not and it doesn't matter because I know now that I can't trust you." Her voice caught and she swallowed hard. "Every time you're not where I think you are or you say something that seems suspicious, I'm going to be right back in that place of disbelief again. I can't go through it. I won't live my life that way anymore."

He shook his head, the sting of her words digging straight into his soul. "Laura—"

"I think I've fallen in love with you, Colton, and that's what makes this so difficult. I want nothing more than to fall into your arms and let you whisk me back to the ranch because it's come to feel more like a home to me than my own home. But I can't do it. I'm sorry. I won't do it."

Laura shut the door in his face before he could offer another protest, leaving him dumbfounded and standing on the porch uncertain what to do. She'd said she loved him and his heart wanted to whoop for joy, but it was tempered by the finality of her last words. She loved him, but she couldn't—she wouldn't—be with him.

He knew what he had to do. It didn't matter that she wasn't at his ranch anymore. This was just another location. He wasn't abandoning her, though. Somehow, someway, he was going to keep her safe. She might not want his protection, but she was going to get it regardless. He'd made a vow to keep her safe and he intended to do just that.

Laura was torn. She was grateful for Miranda's help, but she was devastated and heartbroken that another person in her life had let her down. Why did everyone in her life disappoint her?

Miranda entered the living room carrying a tray with two cups of steaming coffee. "I'm so sorry this happened to you, Laura. Maybe I shouldn't have told you. I feel as if I betrayed Blake's confidence by telling you, but I thought you had a right to know."

"I appreciate you telling me," Laura said. "And thank you for letting me stay here."

"Of course."

Laura sipped her coffee, noting an odd aftertaste. It tasted bitter, but she assumed that was the creamer Miranda had used.

Miranda chattered on, but Laura found her attention waning. Her eyes grew heavy and her hand unsteady. She placed her coffee cup on the table and interrupted Miranda.

"I have her," Miranda stated. "She's at my house nd she's been subdued." She rattled off the address nd then finished with harsh words. "Don't forget to ring my money."

Laura kept struggling as the last vestiges of energy seeped from her limbs. She lay on the stairs, realizing escape was futile at this point. She'd been played. Betrayed in the worst possible way. She'd trusted Miranda and the woman had taken advantage of her.

She'd once again put her faith in the wrong person.

Colton slammed the door of the truck and got out at the sheriff's office. The place was a buzz of activity, people running around grabbing equipment. They looked on high alert. Blake was shouting orders and referring to a map on the table as a group of deputies listened intently.

"What's going on?" Colton asked his friend when the deputies scattered.

Blake pulled on his protective vest and checked his gun. "The FBI just issued a fugitive alert for Randall. He was spotted less than thirty miles from Compton nd heading this way. We're setting up checkpoints at ll areas of entry into town." He looked at Colton and bviously saw the discouraged look on his face. "What's rong with you?"

"She left me," he said and Blake nodded knowingly.

"Miranda told me. I'm sorry, Colton. Miranda re- y cares about Laura," Blake assured him. "Ever since y first met, they've become close friends. Miranda

"I'm suddenly feeling very tired. I think
stairs and lie down."

"Sure," Miranda stated.

Laura stood. Her head was woozy and she ne
back, losing her balance. She didn't understa
she was suddenly so sleepy. She walked to the
and tripped on the first one, falling and landing
steps. The room seemed to spin and her gaze fal
What was happening?

She looked up to see Miranda standing over her,
her face a haze of weird angles and distortions. Laura
reached out to her.

"What's happening to me?" she managed to ask.

In her delirium, Miranda seemed to be standing over
her with a smile on her face. Her gaze was intensive but
not at all worried. In fact, she appeared to be…gloating.

A sudden realization hit Laura. Miranda had tricked
her. She had been the one to tell her things about Colt
Were they even true? She'd taken her in, given he
place to stay and given her…coffee. With dawning
ror, she suddenly knew exactly what was happeni
her. She had all the symptoms—unexplained dr
ness and loss of equilibrium. She'd been drugge

She reached out her hand to find somethin
thing, that could help her all the while angry at
for believing Miranda's lies. She'd distrusted
She'd hurt Colton for no reason.

"He can't help you now," Miranda whispe
room began to fade.

As if from a tunnel, she heard the other
numbers, then speak to someone.

is always asking me about Laura and how we're going to protect her. She'll look out for her."

"I shouldn't have hidden my past from her. I should have been up front about it from the start."

"If you had, she just would have left sooner."

"I never lied to her. Never." He scrubbed a weary hand down his face. "I just never told her the whole truth."

"You're wrong, Colton. You did lie to her. You misrepresented yourself and you know you did. And don't give me that 'who me?' look. The truth is that you never thought you were good enough for her. You thought your past was something that had to remain hidden."

"Given Laura's situation, absolutely."

"Well, you were wrong, my friend. She needed to know the real you and the real you includes your past, thorns and all."

Colton shook his head. "She would only have left sooner and then Randall would have gotten his hooks into her."

"You don't know that. For all your big talk about trust, you didn't trust her, either."

He narrowed his eyes and a muscle flexed in his jaw. "What are you talking about?"

"You didn't trust her to believe in you. You can't see past your own mistakes to let Laura see the real you. You're not perfect, Colton. Frankly, you're hardheaded and more stubborn than any person I've ever known. But you've got so many great qualities, as well." Blake shrugged. "Fact is, you can't truly know a person unless you know the good *and* the bad about them. You kept a part of yourself from Laura and that wasn't right."

Hard as it was to admit, he knew the sheriff had a point. He'd been wrong to keep his past from Laura. But now she knew and look how she'd reacted.

"What do I do now?"

"What you vowed to do. Protect her. I have officers blocking the roads into town and I told Miranda to make sure the doors were locked and the alarm was set. The McGowens blindsided her before, but she knows how to protect herself." He reached out and clapped a hand on his friend's shoulder. "Trust me, she'll keep Laura safe."

Colton knew Blake was right, but every instinct demanded that he burst into that house and carry Laura back to the safety of the ranch, where he could keep his own two eyes on her. However, for once, he was going to listen to reason.

Laura heard sounds as consciousness seeped back into her. Before she opened her eyes, she realized she couldn't move. Something was preventing her from moving her hands. She opened her eyes and saw that she was tied to a kitchen chair. Her hands and feet were bound with duct tape.

Her head was heavy. She knew it was from the drugs. Whatever Miranda had given her, she wondered if she'd given her too much.

Miranda was sitting at the kitchenette nonchalantly flipping through a fashion magazine and drinking from a can of cola. She looked up and saw Laura was waking.

She sighed. "It's about time you woke up. For a while there I thought I might have given you too much."

"You drugged me," Laura accused.

Miranda's tone had a hint of annoyance as if she was bored with Laura stating the obvious. "Yes, I know. I'm the one who did it."

"What did you give me?"

"Neurontin. Blake takes it for his back. I figured he wouldn't miss a few pills."

Her mind was a jumbled mess, but she wondered if Blake was in on this with Miranda.

"Why are you doing this?" Laura asked. She vaguely remembered Miranda on the phone before she'd passed out, talking with someone, telling them she had Laura and demanding money.

"It's all about the money, Laura. I need it so I can get out of his backward, good-for-nothing town."

"But you and Blake—"

"I thought I was going to marry a soldier and travel the world. But then the ambush happened and Blake came running back to this little hick town. And he expects me to live here with him for good. Can you imagine that?" She scoffed. "*Me?* Stay here? The only thing that's been keeping me here is I haven't had the money to leave. Now, thanks to you, I can finally escape this place."

Her laughter was full of coarse bitterness that made Laura's heart break for Blake. He had no idea the contempt Miranda held for him.

"Thanks to me?" She thought she knew Miranda's plan, was horrified at what she was sure she knew was right. "What…what did you do, Miranda? Who did you call earlier?"

"Why, Chuck Randall, of course. He promised me a boatload of money to get you away from Colton."

"You were behind it all, weren't you? You turned off the alarm. You hired those men to come after me. It was all you, wasn't it?"

"That's right. I realized quickly who you were. Mr. Sheedy—I believe you met him at the store the first day we met—is a client at my employer's law office. I ran into him at the store that day and he told me all about the reward that was being offered. I confess I was curious at first. Then I saw how much the reward was. So I made plans with the McGowen cousins— also clients, as you know—to split the reward, but they messed everything up. Incompetents," she hissed in disgust. "Finally I struck a deal with Randall. Assured him I could get you away from Colton. And so I did."

Laura heard the sound of a car approaching the house. Miranda stood and glanced out the window, then smiled. "He's here. I'm about to be stinking rich."

Fear shot through her. "Miranda, you have no idea what Randall is capable of. Don't you even care what he's going to do to me? He'll kill me. He'll kill us both!"

Miranda leaned down, smiled, then tore a strip of duct tape and fastened it over Laura's mouth. "Do you want to know what your problem is, sweetie? You're a victim. You allow people to walk all over you. I make things happen. That's the difference between you and me."

Laura couldn't believe the coldness in Miranda's

eyes. She'd thought she knew her, but now she realized she'd never known the true woman. Miranda couldn't care less what Randall might do to Laura. All she cared about was herself. Miranda was the true definition of selfishness.

A banging on the door caused them both to look up.

Laura's heart raced as fear rippled through her. Randall was going to have her. He would force her to marry him and then in all likelihood she would be killed. Perhaps tortured first or kept prisoner, but eventually killed once Randall tired of her and convinced himself he could indeed have whatever or whoever he wanted.

Miranda rushed to the door and pulled it open. Laura tensed as Randall stepped inside. He spotted her in the chair and a sly grin formed on his face that sent shivers through her. She struggled to free her arms and legs, pulling against the tape.

"Welcome," Miranda said. "Did you have any trouble getting here?"

"No, not much. The police were setting up roadblocks, but I managed to sneak through before they were completely established. Also, I had to take care of the officer parked across the street standing watch."

He was talking about killing a police officer as if he'd just knocked down her mailbox instead of murdering someone. The man truly was a maniac. Laura's mind went to Colton and she realized she would never see him again. The last words she'd said to him had been angry and bitter. She'd called him untrustworthy, but he wasn't. She'd been tricked and now she might never see him again to tell him how wrong she'd been about him.

Fear lashed through her and Laura longed for the ability to scream as Randall knelt beside her. He reached out and stroked her arm. His touch felt vile and made her physically ill. She looked away from him to Miranda, who was still gloating over her brilliant plan.

"You did it," Randall said and Miranda smiled.

"I told you I could get her away from Colton. It was easy."

Randall stood and looked down at her. "Yes, you did. You did good. You accomplished what my own people weren't able to accomplish."

Her face turned hard. "Now, about our arrangement. I want my money."

Laura wanted to scream at her to be careful, not to confront him directly, but they both ignored her grunts. The tape over her mouth prevented her warning from getting through. Randall was a dangerous man and she could see Miranda thought she was the one in charge. Laura knew better, though. Randall never let anyone play games with him.

He picked up a bag he'd dropped by the door and handed it to her. "It's what we agreed upon."

Miranda took the bag, her eyes widening. "Wow, that's a lot of money." She giggled gleefully.

"It's all there. I assure you. But maybe you'd feel better if you counted it."

She opened the bag and pulled out a handful of money, a big grin spreading across her face. Miranda seemed satisfied at selling Laura out. Laura knew she should be angry, but she was only sad. Miranda had no idea who she was dealing with. Randall was lethal, and the fact that he'd come himself didn't bode well for either Miranda or Laura.

As she was basking in her newfound wealth, Randall showed his true colors. He pulled a gun and pointed it at Miranda. She seemed surprised when she saw it.

"What are you doing? We had a deal."

"I'm altering our deal," Randall told her. Then he pulled the trigger.

Miranda jumped, then bent over. She grabbed the back of the chair as she slowly fell to her knees. Fear and shock rippled through Laura. He'd just shot the woman right in front of her.

Laura struggled against her binds, screaming against the tape over her mouth. All she wanted was to run far away from this maniac, but as she looked at Miranda slumped on the floor, blood pooling around her, she knew she needed help or she would die.

Randall put away the gun and retrieved his bag of money from the table. "I'll be right back," he said as he walked out the door.

Laura tried to scoot her chair toward Miranda. The woman's face had grown pale and still. She was losing blood fast. Laura pulled again at her restraints. If only she could get free, she could try to help.

Miranda's eyes moved her way, but they were the only things that moved.

Laura pulled and pulled until her chair tipped over and the tape gave way. She yanked her hand free, then freed herself from the other tape. She scrambled over to Miranda, dragging the chair behind her, a last remnant of the duct tape still clinging to her.

She tried to glance at the wound, but blood was gushing so fast. Laura looked around for something to place against it, grabbing a dish towel and placing it over the wound.

"It's going to be okay," Laura assured her. "You're going to be fine. Where's your phone?"

Laura groped for the phone, knocking it off the table. As she grabbed for the cell, the door burst open and Randall reappeared. He rushed to Laura and she managed to slip the phone into her pocket. She screamed and tried to fight him, but he quickly overpowered her and dragged her toward the door kicking and screaming. Miranda remained sprawled on the floor, unmoving.

When they got outside, Laura saw that Randall had pulled his car into the garage and the trunk was open. She tried to scream again as he shoved her into the trunk, then leaned down and rebound her hands and feet using the same duct tape Miranda had used on her. He tore off one additional piece of duct tape and placed it over her mouth. She was in trouble. Real trouble. As the trunk slammed shut, Laura was left with a deep, sinking feeling that she would probably never see the light of day again and she wished more than anything that she'd never left Colton's side.

It had been dumb to leave Colton. She'd acted impulsively and without even giving him a chance to explain. Yes, she'd been hurt at learning about his past and more so by the fact that he'd hidden it from her. But in that pivotal moment, she'd made a grievous error. She'd lost her faith in him, decided he was someone she could no longer count on. That was why she'd believed

Miranda's lies so easily. But the fact was Colton had been there for her from the start. He'd seen her struggle and stepped in to help even when it would have been easier to walk away. He'd taken a chance on her and she'd let him down.

Oh, how she yearned to talk to him one more time. She wanted to tell him how sorry she was and how she wished she could take back all the ugly words she'd said to him. She wanted—she needed—to apologize to him. She owed him that much.

Laura struggled with the binds and hot tears flooded her eyes. She had no one now. She'd run from Colton and now he had no way to know where she was or to know she was in trouble. But she still had God and He knew where she was and what was going to happen to her. Would He intervene to save her? She didn't know. She certainly didn't deserve His intervention or His mercy, but that hadn't stopped Him from sending His son to the cross to die for her sin.

She tried to focus on that. God had this situation in His hands, and no matter what happened to her, He would be with her.

She knew her death would kill Colton. He would feel as though he'd failed her, but it wasn't his fault she'd run off. It wasn't his fault she'd been tricked by Miranda into believing lies about him. If only she'd trusted more, trusted in Colton completely, then none of this would have happened. She'd realized too late that it was her own distrust that had done her in.

God, watch over him, she prayed. *Keep him safe*

*and help him to understand that this wasn't his fault.
It was mine.*

Hope sprang anew as she heard and felt the car
stop, the door open and shut, then voices. She realized quickly they were at a police barricade. If they
had roadblocks set up, then that must mean that they
were looking for her. She tried to scream for help but
couldn't, struggled to move around and kick her legs,
anything to make enough noise to alert those outside
that she was in the trunk.

Her heart lurched and she attempted to cry out when
the driver's door opened and closed again. Her hope
faded as the roar of the engine kicked to life and the
car sped away.

Dread settled into her and she grew still. Randall had
done it again. He'd obviously talked his way through a
roadblock that she knew had been set up to catch him.

The man really was bulletproof.

Colton waited at the main checkpoint into town along
with Blake. He checked in with all the officers at the
roadblocks set up around town. No one had had a visual of Randall or the car he'd been seen driving. Blake
had shown him the FBI alert. They'd had a confirmed
sighting that indicated Randall was headed to Compton. But that had been hours ago.

Colton's gut was on fire, his instincts telling him
something was wrong. They'd been out here for hours.
How had they missed Randall? Where could he be hiding? And what was his plan? Had he turned around when

he'd seen the roadblocks and hightailed it to another part of the country?

Blake sensed his nervousness and tried to reassure him. "We'll get him, Colton. He won't get out of town."

"I'm less worried about him getting out of town than I am about what he might do while he's in town."

"We've got Compton on lockdown. Don't worry. If he's here, we'll find him."

Colton pulled out his phone and dialed Miranda's number. He just wanted to hear Laura's voice to know she was okay and his worries were unfounded. If she wouldn't give him that, then at least he could get reassurances from Miranda that Laura was safe. But Miranda's phone rang and rang, then finally went to voice mail. He didn't leave a message. She would see the call and know what he wanted and call back.

He tried to busy his mind with coordinating the checkpoints, but after several minutes without a returned call, he dialed the number again. She still didn't answer and the phone went to voice mail.

He shot her a text asking her to let him know they were safe, but she didn't respond to the text, either.

He knew Blake was heading out to the north blockade. He would be busy for a while. Colton grabbed his keys and decided to head to Miranda's house. Anger bit at him. Those women knew the danger Laura was in. It was childish to ignore his calls and texts just because of one little misunderstanding. Laura had to know he only had her best interest in mind. He stopped, reminding himself that she didn't believe that. But he'd made a vow to protect her, and regardless of what she thought of him, he was going to live up to it.

He pulled up to Miranda's house, hopped out of the truck and approached the porch. He knocked but heard no movement from inside and no one came to answer. He knocked again, this time louder. They were probably upstairs and hadn't heard him.

"Miranda, it's Colton," he hollered. "I'm only here to make sure you're both okay."

He listened intently but still didn't hear any movement from inside.

Was it possible they were hiding from him? He didn't think Miranda would. She was much more the in-your-face type. Besides, Blake's fiancée knew he would never do anything to harm Laura.

He glanced in through the window again. The curtain obscured his view, but he didn't see anyone moving around. Had they left the house?

He hopped off the porch and walked to the garage. He knew the code to open the door from when he'd helped Blake install the new garage door. He punched the code into the keypad and waited as the door rumbled up.

Fear shot through him when he saw the car parked inside. Not Miranda's Nissan Maxima, but a silver Lexus with River City casino emblems. This was the car Randall had been spotted in. He rushed into the garage and looked inside the car. It was empty, but what was it doing here in the first place and where was Miranda's car?

He hurried to the door leading into the house from

the garage. Through the window he spotted a figure on the kitchen floor. A hand, unmoving, and what looked like blood around it. He tried the knob and found it locked, so he put his shoulder into the door and rammed it. It burst open and he rushed inside toward the figure and saw it was Miranda. Her blond hair was discolored from the blood spilled around her. He pressed on her neck for a pulse but found none. She was dead. His gut clenched both with sadness for Miranda and fear for Laura.

He rushed through the house calling her name even though his gut told him she was already gone. She was more than likely with Randall, traveling in Miranda's car undetected. He searched upstairs, but as he suspected, she wasn't there, either. He raked a frantic hand through his hair. Miranda was dead and Laura was gone.

Part of him wanted nothing more than to lie down and cry, but he wouldn't. It wasn't him. He was a ranger to the core and he had a job to do. Laura was still out there and he wouldn't rest until he found her.

The call to Blake was one of the hardest Colton had ever had to make. Other Compton officers were already on scene when Blake's patrol car roared up the drive.

Colton saw him leap from his car and run to the house. He stopped him at the porch. "Are you sure you want to see her?"

Blake's eyes shot fire at Colton and he stepped aside. He'd known what the answer would be, but he'd had to ask, even if only to slow Blake down. He was about to experience one of the most devastating scenes he would ever face, possibly even worse than the night of the ambush.

Colton followed him inside. Two officers stopped him at the kitchen door.

"You can't go in," one said. "We have to preserve the scene."

He pushed them away and stepped inside anyway, but Colton could see he was being careful as he stood over the body and stared.

Colton turned away from the scene to give him privacy. The other two officers had a duty to make sure he didn't disrupt any evidence, but Colton's only duty was to his friend.

When Blake emerged from the kitchen, he was pale and forlorn. He held on to the wall for support, then managed to compose himself. His face turned hard and Colton recognized his ranger get-things-done face. They'd all had one. It was the expression they made when terrible events occurred but they still had to carry on and complete the mission.

"He has Miranda's car?"

"Yes," Colton answered. "I figure he thought it'd make it easier to slip out of town in her car than his own, which he knew everyone was looking for."

"We need to alert the checkpoints."

"Already done, Blake," one of the officers stated. "Everyone in town knows Miranda's car and they've all been alerted to watch for it."

"Does it have GPS tracking?" Colton asked.

Blake shook his head. "No, it's an older model. No GPS."

"What about her cell phone?" Colton asked. He looked at the two officers. "Did you find her cell phone?"

"No. We haven't found it."

"Miranda always had her cell phone with her. It was practically glued to her hand," Blake said.

"I've been calling and texting it for hours with no answer. Maybe Laura grabbed it before Randall abducted her. If she was able to hide it from him, it might still be with her."

Blake took out his phone. "She's on my cell phone plan and I have the locate-my-phone app."

Colton looked over his shoulder as Blake navigated through the app. A locator map came up, a blinking blue dot indicating a position.

"It's definitely not in the house," he said. He fidgeted with the settings and the map expanded.

The blue dot appeared to be moving along the old Braxton Highway. "There it is!" Colton exclaimed. "She must have taken the phone."

"Or Randall took it. Either way, we can track their movement." Blake turned to the two officers, his expression hard and determined. "You stay here and preserve the scene. Call me if anything comes up."

"Will do," they said.

Colton rushed out to his truck. Blake stopped at his squad car and opened the trunk, pulling out his shotgun. He glanced at Colton as he pulled on his bulletproof vest. "You have your vest?"

Colton nodded. "In the truck."

"I think you're going to need it."

Colton got into the car with him and Blake took off. He could tell that his friend was hurting on the inside, and the next few months would be long and difficult for him, but Colton instinctively knew Blake was also now on the hunt for justice, and if that justice meant taking out Randall, then he was just the man to do it.

Laura managed to back up against something hard and metal. Although she had no idea what it was, it had an edge to it that she could use to tear the tape around her wrists. She rubbed against the edged piece until she felt the tape begin to give. Finally she heard it rip and was able to pull her hands apart. She pulled off the tape over her mouth and around her feet, then fumbled around for the cell phone she'd stashed in her pocket.

Hope soared through her when she found it. She pressed the button and saw that it was working. There were also six missed calls and a text message from Colton. It pained her to know he must be thinking she was ignoring his call.

She quickly dialed and the phone rang once, then twice, until finally Colton's frantic voice answered.

"Laura, where are you? Are you hurt?"

Tears sprang to her eyes at the sound of his voice. He'd assumed she was calling, which meant they'd obviously found Miranda's body. "I'm okay," she whispered. "I'm in the trunk of the car, but I managed to sneak Miranda's phone with me."

"We're tracking you by that phone. Do you know where you are?"

"No, I can't see anything. I'm scared. Miranda—"

"We know," Colton told her in a soft, soothing voice. "We're coming to get you, darlin'. Just hang on."

The brake lights flashed red and Laura heard the squeak of the brakes. "We're stopping." She heard the door open and the crunch of feet approaching the trunk. "He's coming." She scooted herself farther back as the trunk opened and Randall looked inside. Laura slid the phone behind her so he wouldn't see it.

"So you managed to untie yourself, did you?" He reached in, grabbed her and hauled her out of the car.

Laura screamed and dropped the phone, but Colton's voice came through loud and clear.

"Laura! What's happening?"

Randall heard it and reached for the phone. "How did you manage to sneak this past me?" He put his ear to the phone and listened as Colton demanded he let her go. Randall's face darkened.

"You thought you could put one over on me, Laura? You called your boyfriend to come after me?" He raised his hand, then smacked her hard across the face. She cried out and fell against the car. Pain ripped through her head and blinded her for a moment. She pulled herself to her feet just in time to see Randall use his boot to smash the phone, effectively cutting off Colton's angry tirade of promises of what he would do to Randall when he found him.

Her abductor grinned, satisfied he'd ended that problem. He slammed the trunk closed, then grabbed her by the arms and pulled her with him.

"Don't try anything else like that," he warned, pulling his gun on her.

Laura reluctantly went with him. She glanced back at the phone and wondered if that would be the last time she ever heard Colton's voice.

NINE

The phone call ended abruptly. The last thing he'd heard was the sound of Laura frightened and in pain. What had Randall done to her?

"He found the phone."

Fear raged through him. He might lose Laura. It was more real at this moment than it had ever been. He was at a loss to help her. She might die and there might be nothing he could do to stop it.

He'd never felt so powerless in his entire life.

Blake glanced at his own phone. "And we just lost our tracking capability."

"At least we still know we're heading in the right direction."

Blake pulled over and together they looked over a map of the area. "We know that he was heading to this particular area. The routes out of town are blocked off, so he must be hiding out somewhere."

Colton tapped a finger against his chin, considering. If Randall couldn't get out of town, he would try to find somewhere to hunker down. Colton studied the map closely, looking for anything, anyplace, Randall might use for a hideout. Then it hit him. He scanned the area again, finally singling out one particular place.

"The old drive-in movie theater. It's private and doesn't get a lot of traffic. And it's in this direction."

Blake spoke into his radio, instructing his men to where he and Colton were headed.

He drove to the drive-in and pulled off to the side of the road. Colton got out and went to the trunk. After withdrawing several weapons, he slipped on a protective vest. He had the same feeling now as he used to before missions, and although he was glad to have Blake by his side, he wished his other ranger brothers were there, as well. But this had all gone down so quickly, there hadn't been time to call on them.

Exhaling slowly, Colton squared his shoulders, bracing himself for what lay ahead. One way or another, Laura was coming out of there alive. Randall was a different story. It was his choice whether or not he lived through this.

Randall dragged Laura through a clearing toward what looked like an abandoned building. She saw the big outdoor movie screen and realized they were at the abandoned drive-in Colton had told her about.

He kicked in the door to the building, then pushed Laura inside and shut the door. She landed on top of a stack of metal bins, which went crashing to the floor with a loud clank.

He growled. "You did that on purpose."

"No, I didn't. It was an accident. You shoved me and I fell."

"So it was my fault?" The question burst angrily from him and it seemed he would explode with rage. He lifted his hand, then smacked Laura hard across the face.

She lay still for a moment as the searing pain rippled through her cheek. Then, breathing heavily, she pulled herself to a sitting position. She didn't know what his intention with her was, but she wouldn't cower to him. He would just have to kill her. She wasn't going to give him the satisfaction of being afraid any longer.

She'd never seen Randall look so disheveled and out of control. He looked like a man on the edge and nothing like the power broker she'd known him as.

"What happened to you?" she asked him and he smirked.

"I killed a federal agent today." He must have seen the horror on her face because he nodded. "That's right. He managed to worm his way into my employment only to gather evidence against me. Your friend Miranda is the one who turned me on to his true nature. Before I shot him, he told me the FBI has enough evidence against me to put me in prison for a long time. I believed him about that, so I got out of town as fast as I could."

Laura thought Miranda must have gotten that information about an undercover FBI agent from Blake and it saddened her again to realize how her friend had betrayed those who'd cared about her. His words also seemed to confirm what Colton had told her about going to River City to meet with an undercover FBI agent. He'd told her the truth and she hadn't believed him.

But she had a much bigger problem than Miranda's

betrayal. Randall was, in fact, on the edge. He was losing everything and so he had nothing to lose.

She wasn't going to make it out of there alive.

Her one saving grace was that she'd gotten to speak to Colton before Randall had crushed the phone. She'd been able to hear his voice one final time.

"What do you want from me?" she asked Randall.

He pulled out his gun, pointed it at her, then knelt in front of her, locking eyes with her. "I want to hear you say you love me." When she didn't respond, he cocked the gun and pressed it against her head. "Say it!"

Laura sucked in a breath so full of terror it nearly choked her, but she was determined she wouldn't let Randall win. He wouldn't make her cower. "Is that what you want?" she asked him. "You want me to lie to you? Will a lie make you feel better?"

The gun jerked in his hand, frustration clearly taking over his mind-set. "You'd better say it like you mean it if you know what's good for you." His hand was shaking and she was a little worried the gun might go off by accident.

"You can shoot me, Randall, but you can never make me love you. That's the one thing you can never have."

Her heart already belonged to someone else. He may never be able to forgive her for doubting him and he may not still want her after all this if she survived it, but she loved him and she only hoped to live long enough to tell him so.

Colton checked his weapons. He couldn't afford any misfires, not today, not when Laura's life depended on him. She may never trust him again, but he would still do his best to protect her from Randall.

He glanced over at Blake. His friend was hurting over the loss of Miranda, but Colton knew from experience he would keep his wits about him. He knew the stakes all too well. Randall had already killed an FBI agent and Miranda. He wouldn't hesitate to kill Laura.

Blake took command of the locals who were now arriving, instructing them to set up blockades and establish a perimeter. But Colton doubted it would come to that. Randall wasn't on the run. He was going down and Colton knew from experience he would take anyone and everyone down with him. The fact that he'd come himself for Laura spoke volumes about his intentions. He had plans and no one was getting out of this alive if Randall had his way.

Blake introduced two of his best deputies, both former military who knew how to handle a rifle. "Dunley is a former sniper, so I'm positioning him on the landing at the big screen. Our initial reconnaissance shows they're holed up in the projector booth. That spot should offer a clear view into the building. And this is Waller. He was a marine."

Sniper Dunley gave Colton a reassuring nod of his head. "We'll get her out safely," he said before he left to take his position. Colton summed up the kid—and he was just a kid, probably only twenty-five or twenty-six, the same age as Garrett. He seemed capable, but Colton had never fought with him, never put his trust in the man, and he wished once again that his own team was with him tonight.

"Don't worry," Blake said, obviously sensing his uncertainty. "Dunley is good. He only left the teams because his mother got ill and he had to come home to help care for her. I checked him out when I hired him. He could have had a great career ahead of him had he stayed in the military."

Colton shook off his dread. He didn't have time to go through each man's background to approve or disapprove them. Blake knew his men and Colton trusted his judgment.

Blake motioned toward the map. "I'm putting Johnson, Phillips and Clark to surround the building from each side. I'll take the fourth spot."

He felt better knowing Blake was going in with him. At least he had one of his men backing him, but he was still scared. Everything he wanted out of life was inside that booth.

Quicker than Colton would have thought possible, Dunley's voice came over the radio. "I'm in position and I have a visual. They're definitely in the projector building."

"What do you see?" Blake asked him.

"Laura is crouched in the corner. Randall is pacing back and forth. I see one weapon in his hand, but I can't determine yet if he has more."

"How is Laura?" Colton asked, his voice gruff with emotion. "Is she hurt?"

"She looks frightened but uninjured as far as I can tell, but, guys, this fellow looks unstable. He's waving that gun around."

"I'm going in there," Colton said. All he could think

of, all he could focus on, was getting to her and getting her away from Randall by any means necessary. He started out, but Blake stopped him, placing a hand on his shoulder. "Don't do anything rash, Colton. We need to come up with a plan."

"I have a plan. I'm going in there."

"Don't be dumb, Colton," Blake barked. "We need to figure out how to get the upper hand on him."

Dunley's voice came over the radio again. "He's blocking the windows. I have negative visibility now. He must have made us. Repeat, zero visibility."

"Time to change plans," Blake spoke into his mic. "Looks like we're going to breach the building. Everyone hold for further instructions." He looked at Colton. "Do you remember the Zarneski plan?"

Colton smiled and nodded. "I'm on it."

The Zarneski was a bait-and-switch plan. Basically, one person would keep the target occupied while the other sneaked up behind—or in this case, sneaked past—him to retrieve the girl.

While Blake approached the front of the building, Colton approached the back of the projection shed. The plan was for his buddy to keep Randall busy while Colton figured out a way to get Laura out.

He heard Blake's strong, authoritative voice and was amazed at how controlled it was. His friend continued to amaze him. He honestly didn't know how he was keeping it together.

"Randall, it's Sheriff Michaels. We need to end this."

And then Randall's psychotic response. "Get back! Get back or I'll kill her!"

Colton kept one ear listening to the conversation. He didn't want to be blindsided if Randall suddenly stopped talking or his voice raised, anything indicating he'd reached a boiling point.

Colton climbed stealthily onto the roof, ignoring the pain in his knee, then pried open the ventilation shaft. He slid inside, still cautious of Randall and using his voice to pinpoint where he was in the shed. Sliding in was the dangerous part because he had to use both hands. He was basically unarmed during this process. As soon as his feet hit the floor, his gun was back in his hand.

Laura saw him and jumped up. She started to call out his name, but Colton held his finger to his lips, warning her to remain quiet. She nodded her understanding. He motioned for her to come to him and she did, moving quietly and watching Randall as she did.

Her foot clipped a piece of metal and it clanked to the floor. The noise caused Randall to spin, raise his gun and fire. Colton lunged for Laura, knocking her to the floor. He felt the bullet pierce his flesh beneath his vest and it stung like crazy. Laura's eyes were wide with fear as Colton landed on top of her.

"Get up," Randall commanded. "How dare you try to sneak in here!"

Colton heard the commotion both from outside the building and through his earbud. The gunshot had obviously raised the tension outside among Blake and the others.

He heard Blake's shouts. "Colton, are you okay? What's happening?"

"Get back," Randall hollered to those outside. "Get back or I'll kill them both!"

He closed the distance between them and grabbed Colton by the vest, pulling him off Laura with a crazy unnatural strength obviously fueled by adrenaline.

Colton felt the pain from the gunshot wound rip through him. He stared into Laura's eyes, seeing her fear and worry, and knew he wouldn't be able to do anything about it. Pain blurred his eyes. His balance faltered. And as Randall grabbed him and pulled him off Laura, he slumped and knew he wasn't getting back up.

He'd failed Laura again.

When Laura saw Colton slump onto the floor, a scream ripped through her. She crawled over to him. Blood was gushing from his side. He'd lost a lot of blood in a short of amount of time and she thought Randall's bullet might have nicked an artery. If it had, they had limited time before he bled out. He had to get to a hospital and quickly.

Randall stood over them, gun raised, his face twisted with fury.

Laura pleaded with him for mercy. "He needs to get to a hospital. You have to let his friends come in and get him."

Randall shook his head. "That's not going to happen."

"He'll die,"

"Then he'll die," Randall stated without a bit of empathy in his voice.

Laura had known he was coldhearted, but now she saw it firsthand. He cared about nothing but himself.

Maybe she could use that to get them out of there alive. If Randall wanted her, he could have her if it would save Colton's life.

Colton had come for her. He'd risked his life and might possibly lose it by trying to rescue her despite how she'd treated him. She hadn't trusted him. She'd put them both at risk because she'd believed lies instead of what she'd known in her heart—that she could trust Colton. They were now in this mess because of her. It was her fault. Colton might die because of her foolishness.

She thought about her father. He'd been willing to try to fix the mess but hadn't been able to, and although Laura had appreciated that he'd tried, she hadn't forgiven him for his foolishness. Now she understood how one bad decision could never truly be undone. That was why forgiveness was so important.

But right now she had to do whatever it took to get Colton the help he needed. It was all up to her now.

Blake was still yelling for some kind of communication and she could see it was getting to Randall. He was distracted and confused. She waited until he turned and walked to the window, then saw her opportunity. She took the gun from Colton's hand and aimed it at Randall just as Colton had shown her. This gun was much heavier and it took both hands to hold it at him.

Randall turned and saw it and all the confusion and distraction faded. His face hardened and she knew there was no turning back. She tried her best to keep her hands from shaking, but they still did. She knew she had to stay strong. Focused.

And she found herself praying.

God, please help us. God, please keep Colton alive until we can get him to the hospital. Please help us get out of this mess alive. Make my aim steady and true.

Randall raised his gun and Laura fired. The force of the gun knocked her backward, but she steadied herself. Randall jerked as he was hit, but he swung back to her and she fired again, this time hitting him straight in the chest. He went down and didn't get up.

Suddenly the door burst open and Blake, followed by a swarm of men all dressed in protective gear, their guns raised, filed into the room. Laura made certain not to make any sudden movements until they'd had a moment to process the scene, but she slowly lowered the gun to her side.

Blake stood over Randall. He kicked the gun from his hand and out of reach, then knelt to check for a pulse. He looked at Laura and shook his head, indicating no pulse.

The gun slipped from her hand and clunked against the floor. She wouldn't have been able to explain the emotion that fell over her, but she was sad in a way that she'd killed Randall. She'd never killed anyone before and she'd never even thought about how she would feel afterward if she'd had to do it. And she'd had to shoot him. She knew that. Randall would have surely killed her. He'd already shot Colton.

Colton!

The thought of him pulled her out of her momentary fog and it no longer mattered how it felt to have killed

Randall. She had to focus on the man she loved now and on saving his life.

"What happened?" Blake asked her, following to him.

"Randall shot him." She knelt beside him and pressed her hands into his wound, trying to stem the bleeding. "He's losing blood fast. We have to get him to the hospital."

Blake spoke into his mic. "We need an ambulance in here." He looked at Laura. "They'll be here as fast as they can."

She prayed they made it in time.

Colton began to stir. His eyes fluttered open, but Laura could see they were glassy and unfocused.

"Laura." He spoke her name weakly.

"I'm here. Hold on, Colton," she pleaded. "Help is coming."

"Randall?"

"He can't hurt anyone anymore."

Blake knelt beside him. "He's dead, buddy," Blake said from over her shoulder. "Laura shot him."

Colton reached up and stroked her cheek. "Good girl," he whispered to her.

"I had a good teacher," she said, pressing her face against his hand.

"He's fading," Blake said as Colton's eyes closed and his hand went limp, falling back to his side.

His breathing grew rapid and heavy and he started to sweat. His skin was becoming pale, cold and clammy as blood flow was being directed away.

Laura recognized the symptoms. "He's going into shock," she said hoarsely.

"You're a nurse. Tell me what to do."

"Do you have a medical kit with oxygen?"

"Yes. All our police cruisers come equipped with emergency oxygen kits." He got on the radio and called for someone to bring the kit.

She grabbed Blake's hands and pressed them against the wound in Colton's stomach. "Keep applying pressure."

An officer rushed in with the first-aid kit and Laura reached first for the emergency oxygen. Colton needed an infusion of blood, but for now, oxygen and IV fluids would have to do until they reached the hospital. Realizing she needed to get his blood moving if he had any chance of surviving, she pulled the oxygen mask over his face, then started an IV line and pushed fluids that were also in the emergency kit.

All the while, she kept speaking to Colton, trying to get him to respond to her. "Talk to him," she told Blake. "Tell him to hold on."

In the distance she heard sirens and was relieved the ambulance was finally here.

Blake looked around at all the old furniture and equipment. "It's awfully tight in here. Should we move him?"

Laura shook her head. "Not until the ambulance arrives."

The sirens grew louder until she could hear it right outside the door. Two paramedics burst inside and rushed over to them. Blake moved out of the way, but Laura didn't move.

"I'm an RN. He's sustained a gunshot wound to the abdomen. Excessive bleeding and he's in hypovolemic shock. I've started oxygen and pushed IV fluids, but he's still lethargic and unresponsive."

Laura moved out of the way as the paramedics rolled in a gurney. Blake and another officer helped lift Colton onto the gurney. She stayed by his side as they loaded him into the ambulance. Then she climbed in with them to monitor his vitals.

"I have to stay here to process the scene," Blake said, "but I'll be at the hospital as soon as I can."

"I'll stay with him," she assured him, knowing it must be tearing him up not being able to be with Colton. She knew it would be for her.

"You probably saved his life," the paramedic told her.

She appreciated the sentiment but knew Colton still had a long way to go before he was out of danger.

Her hand shook as she borrowed a stethoscope and checked his heart rate. She couldn't lose him now. He'd risked his life—perhaps even given it—to rescue her. He was a true hero and she couldn't love him more for it.

She placed her hand on his as the ambulance took off and the siren blared. She leaned over him. As a nurse, she'd done all she could do to help him. Besides monitoring his vitals as they made their way to the hospital, there was little she could do. But she could pray. She could pray for God's presence and mercy and forgiveness.

She leaned over Colton and wept, all the emotion she'd been holding back since she'd seen him shot barreling through her.

"God, please place your healing hand on Colton. I love him so much. Don't make him pay the ultimate price for my mistake."

Laura sat in the waiting room at the hospital in River City. Someone had brought her a cold drink and she sipped it absently as she waited for news. Colton had been assessed at the local hospital in Compton, stabilized, then air transported to the more advanced medical facility in River City. Only her status as an RN had allowed her to go with him on the rescue copter. He'd been taken right up to surgery, but the last time she'd seen him, he'd been touch and go. She knew he would be given blood and that would help. She only hoped it wasn't already too late.

Her father had been moved to a regular room, but Denise had loaded him into a wheelchair and pushed him upstairs to wait with his daughter. Laura was thankful to have him with her. All her anger toward him was gone. She felt she understood him a little better now after what she'd been through. Denise stayed with her, too, and Laura was glad. She needed to lean on her friend right now and Denise offered a willing shoulder.

The double doors opened and Blake entered. He looked tired and weary as he approached Laura. She could hardly imagine how he was feeling. He'd lost his fiancée and now faced losing his best friend.

Laura stood as he approached. Worry and grief pressed on his face.

"Have you heard anything?"

"He's still in surgery," she told him.

Blake nodded, then took the seat beside her.

"I'm sorry about Miranda," Laura said.

"Thank you." He took a deep breath. "I need to take your statement officially at some point. I need to know what happened in that house."

She hung her head, wondering how she would tell him. He'd been good to her and he was a good friend to Colton.

"How did Randall get into Miranda's house?" Blake asked her. He must have sensed her hesitancy. "I need the truth, Laura."

"Miranda let him in. She called him."

He stared at her in shock and disbelief. "What?"

"I'm so sorry, Blake. She was going to take the money Randall offered in order to leave town. He double-crossed her and killed her instead."

He shook his head. "No, that's not possible." Blake's shoulders slumped and he buried his face in his hands. "It can't be. She loved me. We had our future planned together."

"I'm so sorry," Laura said softly. She couldn't imagine what he was going through, not only having his fiancée murdered but also discovering she'd betrayed him.

They sat in silence for a while, him nursing his heartbreak and Laura praying for another chance with Colton. Finally the doors opened and a man in scrubs she recognized as the surgeon appeared. Laura leaped to her feet and Blake stood, too.

"How is he?" Laura asked.

"He made it through surgery. The bullet nicked his liver, but we were able to repair the damage. We're going to keep him in ICU for a while, but his prognosis is good."

Laura slumped with relief and thanked God. Colton would survive and that was one obstacle overcome.

But would he ever be able to forgive her for not believing in him? He'd been shot and nearly died trying to rescue her. How could he ever get past that?

Colton heard a beeping sound as he woke up. He pushed his way through to consciousness as the beeping sound increased. He was aware of pain in his abdomen. It stung and itched at the same time. Something had happened. He remembered being shot. The last thing he remembered was Randall shooting him, then turning the gun on Laura.

He jerked awake, his focus now on Laura and getting to her. He realized he was in a hospital. Laura was in the chair beside the bed. His heart lurched, then he slumped back into the bed, pain radiating through him along with adrenaline and relief. He didn't know what had happened, but seeing Laura there beside him was a great relief.

She reached for his hand and he grasped hers.

"I'm so thankful you're safe," he rasped.

"I thought I'd lost you there for a while."

"I'm too stubborn to die," he said, then gave her a wink and smile.

She looked away, then took on a serious tone. "I owe you so much, Colton, but mostly I owe you an apology."

"You don't have anything to apologize for, Laura."

"I should have believed in you, Colton. I should have never doubted you."

He shook his head. He didn't want her carrying around that guilt. "I gave you plenty of reason to doubt me."

"No, that's your past. I got so caught up in judging your past mistakes that I didn't see the man you are now. You're someone I can trust with my life. You shouldn't have had to nearly die to prove that to me."

"I wasn't trying to prove anything."

"I know that. I'm just so sorry you had to pay such a hefty price for my mistake. I allowed Miranda to color my judgment. I didn't trust in what my heart was telling me—that you were the one man I could trust with my life." Her lower lip quivered. "I realized as you were lying near death in that shed that I caused that situation and there will never be anything I can do that will make up for it. I can't change it. All I can do is ask your forgiveness."

He clutched her hand. "I know a thing or two about making mistakes you can't fix. If God can forgive a man like me, I can surely forgive you, Laura. And I do. I've made such a mess of my life and you've been the one good thing in it. I love you, darlin', but I know I come with a lot of baggage. Do you think you can learn to love me despite my past?"

She wiped away tears as she gripped his hand. "I don't even see your past, Colton. It's not who you are anymore. And I already love the man you've become."

His heart soared and he pushed himself up to a sitting position in the bed so he could kiss her. She kissed him back, her lips soft and yielding. Pain ripped through him as he moved wrong and the stitches in his side pulled. He grimaced and Laura pushed away.

"Oh, I'm sorry. I didn't mean to hurt you."

"It's okay," he murmured, pulling her face back to his. "Change always comes with a little pain and sometimes it's a good pain." He touched his lips to hers again and thanked God silently for all His blessings.

EPILOGUE

Colton scratched at the incision on his side and made his way outside with the use of his cane. He felt useless cooped up inside the house as he had been for weeks now. He heard the dogs bark and knew Laura was back from her shift at Compton Medical Center. It was only her second week of work at the new job and he found he missed her being around. She'd taken an apartment in town, but she'd been spending most of her free time at the ranch with him since her official move to Compton.

He walked onto the porch and met her at the truck as she pulled out several bags loaded with groceries. "Can I help?"

"Only by taking it easy," she said with a gently reproving smile. She had obviously stopped off at her new apartment in town to change from her hospital scrubs into jeans and a blouse, and her long hair was loose around her shoulders. He knew she'd had to stop by and take care of her cat, who her friend Denise had found wandering loose and taken home.

"How was your day?"

"It was different, a slower pace than I'm used to, but I like the people I'm working with." She gazed up at him. "But it's a good change. Time to slow down and enjoy life, right?"

"Right," he said, placing a warm kiss on her mouth.

She carried the bags into the kitchen and started putting groceries away. "I saw Blake today. He came into the hospital to take a report on a robbery case."

Colton knew his friend was grieving not only from losing Miranda but also from discovering her deception and scheming. It still burned Colton to think how she'd betrayed all their trust. "How did he look?"

"Tired, but he said he was doing okay."

"He'll get through it. His faith will see him through. Plus, he always has me." He gave her a smile and a wink, and she couldn't help but laugh.

"I also called my father. He's being released from the rehab center next week. I invited him to come spend a few days with me."

He smiled, glad to hear she was making the effort to rebuild the relationship with her father. "I think that's a terrific idea."

He heard a scratch at the front door and opened it. Milo padded across the floor toward Laura and she knelt to pet him.

"Sometimes I think you love that dog more than you love me."

She smiled up at him. "I love you both."

"Well, maybe you can marry him."

"I would, but he hasn't asked me yet," she said, extending the tease.

"Maybe he's just been trying to get up the nerve, afraid you'd say no and laugh him off the face of the earth."

She stood and looked at Colton, a slow smile spreading across her lips. She locked eyes with him as she stated four little words with a determination that made his heart thud against his chest.

"I won't say no."

He couldn't believe this auburn-haired beauty wanted him. He was still in awe of her.

He cleared his throat and prepared to jump into his new life. "I think Milo wants a treat," he told her, motioning at the bag of dog treats on the counter.

She glanced at them curiously, then pulled the bag open. Milo saw them, too, and jumped at her feet. She took one out and tossed it to Milo. The dog lunged for it, jumping up.

Colton watched her and saw her eyes grab onto something.

She scooped Milo up into her arms. "What's this?" she asked, pulling Milo's collar around. She pulled at a piece of string tied around a diamond ring. When she realized what it was, she glanced up at him, tears sparkling in her eyes.

"I can't believe how amazingly blessed I am that you love me, Laura. I can't imagine my life without you. They told me at the hospital that you saved my life. I would have died in that shed if you hadn't intervened. You saved my life in more ways than one and I want to spend the rest of my days on this planet with no one else but you. Will you marry me, darlin', and make me the happiest man that ever lived?"

She pulled off the ring and slipped it onto her finger, then set Milo on the floor. She wrapped her arms around Colton's neck. "I want nothing more out of this life than to be your wife."

He gathered her against him and kissed her tenderly as Milo barked at their feet.

She'd finally found a place to call her forever home.

* * * * *

If you liked this story, pick up these other
RANGERS UNDER FIRE *books*
by Virginia Vaughan.

Nothing's more dangerous than falling in love

YULETIDE ABDUCTION
REUNION MISSION

Available now from Love Inspired!

Find more great reads at www.LoveInspired.com

Dear Reader,

Thanks so much for reading Colton and Laura's story. Forgiveness is a tricky matter. It's one of the most difficult and trying things we as humans have to learn. Laura's life was in a mess because of her father's choices, but it was her own unforgiveness that kept her bound in anger and bitterness and ultimately caused her to lose hope in others. Colton had made mistakes in his past and believed he was beyond redemption in the eyes of man. Fortunately, God had a better plan for both their lives.

This story was a difficult one for me to write because while I was smack in the middle of a story about forgiveness, I found myself in a situation where all I wanted to do was be angry. Like Laura, it was difficult for me to forgive because I didn't feel the one who hurt me deserved forgiveness. Colton's words were a reminder not only to Laura but to me as well, that we forgive because God first forgave us. Laura learned that it was the only way to find hope and happiness again. I pray we all learn that lesson.

I love hearing from my readers! You can contact me through my website, www.virginiavaughanonline.com, or through the publisher.

Virginia

COMING NEXT MONTH FROM
Love Inspired® Suspense

Available September 6, 2016

SEARCH AND RESCUE
Rookie K-9 Unit • by Valerie Hansen
Widowed police chief Ryder Hayes lost his wife to his violent stalker. Now that he's slowly allowing himself to move on and get close to K-9 trainer Sophie Williams, will the killer return to take another woman he cares about?

AGAINST THE TIDE • by Melody Carlson
Inheriting her father's newspaper after his mysterious death, Megan McCallister returns to her coastal hometown—and discovers that someone wants *her* dead, too. But with the help of Garret Larsson, she's determined to finish her father's final story...and expose his killer.

PLAIN TRUTH
Military Investigations • by Debby Giusti
After someone attacks pediatrician Ella Jacobsen in her clinic for Amish children, Special Agent Zach Swain investigates—and promises to keep her safe. But for Zach, searching for the would-be killer could mean losing his heart.

WITNESS PURSUIT
Echo Mountain • by Hope White
When property manager Cassie McBride finds a dead body in a rental cabin, she enters the killer's crosshairs. And police chief Nate Walsh makes it his mission to protect her—even at the risk of his own life.

BREACH OF TRUST • by Jodie Bailey
A hacker is out to get ex-soldier Meghan McGuire. And she must reunite with her former partner, Tate Walker—the man she once loved but thought was dead—to ensure her safety.

COUNTDOWN • by Heather Woodhaven
When Rachel Cooper saves her neighbor's twins from a kidnapping, James McGuire's enemies target her. Someone planted a weapon on his company's soon-to-launch satellite—and they'll use anyone close to him as leverage to keep him from stopping its scheduled takeoff.

LISCNM0816

REQUEST YOUR FREE BOOKS!

2 FREE RIVETING INSPIRATIONAL NOVELS PLUS 2 FREE MYSTERY GIFTS

Love Inspired®
SUSPENSE
RIVETING INSPIRATIONAL ROMANCE

YES! Please send me 2 FREE Love Inspired® Suspense novels and my 2 FREE mystery gifts (gifts are worth about $10). After receiving them, if I don't wish to receive any more books, I can return the shipping statement marked "cancel." If I don't cancel, I will receive 4 brand-new novels every month and be billed just $4.99 per book in the U.S. or $5.49 per book in Canada. That's a savings of at least 17% off the cover price. It's quite a bargain! Shipping and handling is just 50¢ per book in the U.S. and 75¢ per book in Canada.* I understand that accepting the 2 free books and gifts places me under no obligation to buy anything. I can always return a shipment and cancel at any time. Even if I never buy another book, the two free books and gifts are mine to keep forever.

123/323 IDN GH5Z

Name	(PLEASE PRINT)

Address	Apt. #

City	State/Prov.	Zip/Postal Code

Signature (if under 18, a parent or guardian must sign)

Mail to the **Reader Service:**
IN U.S.A.: P.O. Box 1867, Buffalo, NY 14240-1867
IN CANADA: P.O. Box 609, Fort Erie, Ontario L2A 5X3

**Are you a current subscriber to Love Inspired® Suspense books and want to receive the larger-print edition?
Call 1-800-873-8635 or visit www.ReaderService.com.**

* Terms and prices subject to change without notice. Prices do not include applicable taxes. Sales tax applicable in N.Y. Canadian residents will be charged applicable taxes. Offer not valid in Quebec. This offer is limited to one order per household. Not valid for current subscribers to Love Inspired Suspense books. All orders subject to credit approval. Credit or debit balances in a customer's account(s) may be offset by any other outstanding balance owed by or to the customer. Please allow 4 to 6 weeks for delivery. Offer available while quantities last.

Your Privacy—The Reader Service is committed to protecting your privacy. Our Privacy Policy is available online at www.ReaderService.com or upon request from the Reader Service.

We make a portion of our mailing list available to reputable third parties that offer products we believe may interest you. If you prefer that we not exchange your name with third parties, or if you wish to clarify or modify your communication preferences, please visit us at www.ReaderService.com/consumerschoice or write to us at Reader Service Preference Service, P.O. Box 9062, Buffalo, NY 14240-9062. Include your complete name and address.

LIS15

SPECIAL EXCERPT FROM

Love Inspired.
SUSPENSE

Desert Valley's new police chief must hunt down the woman terrorizing his town and keep her from hurting the dog trainer he's coming to care for.

Read on for an excerpt from
SEARCH AND RESCUE,
the exciting conclusion to the series
ROOKIE K-9 UNIT.

"I'm going to make a quick run to town and back," Sophie told newly minted police chief Ryder Hayes and noted his scowl in response.

"Be careful. You may have been a cop once," Ryder said, "but you're a dog trainer now."

That was a low blow. Sophie clenched her jaw.

"We all have to be on guard," he said. "There's no telling where Carrie is or whether she's through killing people."

"I agree with you. I'll keep my eyes open," Sophie said.

He arched a brow. "Are you carrying?"

"Of course." She patted a flat holster clipped inside the waist of her jeans. "I won't be out and about for long. I'm going to the train station to pick up a dog."

"Why didn't you say so in the first place?"

She was still smiling a few minutes later when she parked at the small railroad station and climbed out of her official K-9 SUV.

A sparse crowd was beginning to disembark as she approached. She shaded her eyes. *There!* A slim young police cadet had stepped down and turned, tugging on a leash. "Hello! I've been expecting you. I'm Sophie Williams."

"This is Phoenix," the young man said, indicating the silver, black and white Australian shepherd cowering at his feet. "I hope you have better success with him than we did."

She grasped the end of the leash, gave it slack and took several steps back. She politely bade him goodbye, turned and walked away with Phoenix at her side.

"Heel," Sophie ordered.

The dog refused to budge.

She faced him. "What is it, boy? What's scaring you?"

A loud bang echoed a fraction of a second later. Sophie recognized a rifle shot and instinctively ducked.

The dog surged toward her. She opened her arms to accept him just as a second shot was fired. Together they scrambled for safety behind her SUV.

Don't miss
SEARCH AND RESCUE by Valerie Hansen,
available wherever
Love Inspired® Suspense books and ebooks are sold.

www.LoveInspired.com

SPECIAL EXCERPT FROM

Love Inspired

*When Esther Stoltzfus's childhood crush,
Nathaniel Zook, returns to their Amish community
and asks for help with his farm—and an orphaned
boy in need—will their friendship blossom
into a happily-ever-after?*

*Read on for a sneak preview of
HIS AMISH SWEETHEART by Jo Ann Brown,
available September 2016 from Love Inspired!*

"Are you sure you want Jacob to stay with you?" Esther asked.

"I'm sure staying at my farm is best for him now," Nathaniel said. "The boy needs something to do to get his mind off the situation, and the alpacas can help."

Nathaniel held his hand out to assist Esther onto the seat of the buggy.

She regarded him with surprise, and he had to fight not to smile. Her reaction reminded him of Esther the Pester from their childhood, who'd always asserted she could do anything the older boys did…and all by herself.

Despite that, she accepted his help. The scent of her shampoo lingered in his senses. He was tempted to hold on to her soft fingers, but he released them as soon as she was sitting. He was too aware of the *kinder* and other women gathered behind her.

She picked up the reins and leaned toward him. "If it becomes too difficult for you, bring him to our house."

"We'll be fine." At that moment, he meant it. When her bright blue eyes were close to his, he couldn't imagine being anything but fine.

Then she looked away, and the moment was over. She slapped the reins and drove the wagon toward the road. He watched it go. A sudden shiver ran along him. The breeze was damp and chilly, something he hadn't noticed while gazing into Esther's pretty eyes.

The sound of the rattling wagon vanished in the distance, and he turned to see Jacob standing by the fence, his fingers through the chicken wire again in the hope an alpaca would come to him. The *kind* had no idea of what could lie ahead for him.

Take him into Your hands, Lord. He's going to need Your comfort in the days to come. Make him strong to face what the future brings, but let him be weak enough to accept help from us.

Taking a deep breath, Nathaniel walked toward the boy. He'd agreed to take care of Jacob and offer him a haven at the farm. Now he had to prove he could.

Don't miss
HIS AMISH SWEETHEART by Jo Ann Brown,
available September 2016 wherever
Love Inspired® books and ebooks are sold.

www.LoveInspired.com